I0575117

A NIGEL GRANT NOVEL

AT FACE VALUE

ROBERT LOUIS HESSLINK

Published in the United States of America by
Hesslink Publishing, Damascus, Oregon

Print ISBN: 978-1-7353291-1-6
eBook ISBN: 978-1-7353291-0-9

Cover design by Jeanine Henning
Book design by Maureen Cutajar, www.gopublished.com

To Mom and Dad

ACKNOWLEDGMENTS

I am grateful for the input and support of my brother Charlie and his wife, Trish, who took the time to read several early versions, which I admit were a long way from this final product.

I am thankful that my friend, Steve Siegel, took the time to read and provide constructive feedback on the plot, the characters, and the nonsense in those early versions. And, to the many friends who offered support and insights along the way.

It goes without saying that I am grateful and appreciative of my awesome spouse, Kit, who didn't question my announcement of wanting to write this book, and who gave me that initial spark to continue when she said, "It's good," after reading the first 120 pages. Her guidance on everything grammatical and her attention to detail always make anything I write of better quality.

Nigel matured through the course of this writing, but he never changed. And, for that I am thankful, because in creating Nigel Grant, I wanted a character that was tangible and vulnerable. Not a super-hero but a guy just like any other guy or gal that ventures through life on this wonderful planet, without the slightest idea of their impact on those around them.

PROLOGUE

Present day
March 12, 2021
Flying to Austin, Texas

"Sir." A long sigh… "Sir?"

"Nigel, wake up. She wants to know what you want to eat," comments my seatmate.

I look up at the flight attendant. Nice looking babe. Short, blonde hair with green eyes looking at me through the custom American Airlines face shield.

"Chicken, I will have the chicken and some white wine, please," I say to the flight attendant.

New federal guidelines due to the coronavirus pandemic allow individuals to decide on their own about how to best protect themselves, but it is surprising to see that she is wearing a face shield. They are so cumbersome and clunky. I guess the old saying, "better safe than sorry" still applies.

"Sorry, but we're out of chicken."

"Fine, I'll take the beef dish and red wine, Cabernet, if you have it. Please," I say.

I can't quite place the six-point facial alignment that I need for full identification, but she does seem to exhibit face characteristics that are consistent with our database. I smile, taking the time to get a good look at her beautiful green eyes, before deciding whether I need to report her for further identification by our surveillance team. This trip is my first chance to use my face recognition training for my new job.

Traditionally, face recognition uses a six-point biometric system that consists of the eyes, nose, chin, and ears. But ever since the COVID-19 pandemic last year, the world of face recognition has been turned upside down with the use of masks, scarves, and even these shields.

The flight attendant nods and moves on towards the back of the plane.

My seatmate, Clare, comments through her face covering, "Jesus, Nigel, why do you always have to be such a pain?"

"Oh, I don't know, I thought asking for a Cabernet was a reasonable request," I say looking at Clare.

I still haven't gotten used to her wearing a face cover. She isn't in any one of the at-risk categories, but that hasn't diminished her enthusiasm for being cautious. Personally, I don't bother to wear one anymore. I just don't feel the necessity.

I learned during my training sessions at Face Value that a person's face can be altered by a variety of means. Cosmetic surgery is the most common with aging close behind. However, ever since the coronavirus outbreak, people have been using face masks or face coverings for protection along with sunglasses and hats, which presents a problem for law enforcement. Who is wearing it for personal protection and who is wearing it to hide from surveillance?

Most of the time the uncertainty doesn't require the involvement of our surveillance team, which I think is the case for the flight attendant. But, the guy up in first class offers a completely different challenge. He isn't wearing a face mask, and I am pretty certain that his face is not in our database. I'll have to check him out a little more carefully when we land.

"I gotta pee," Clare pushes up my tray and rushes past me, not giving me time to make room. But, then again, looking at her butt reminds me of a time when I focused on things other than faces.

Clare returns ranting about the line for the restroom and the lack of amenities, which I think means toilet paper.

"How'd it go?" I say.

"How come they can't build bigger bathrooms in these wide-body jets? Here it is 2021 and with all the technology in the world, they skimp on bathrooms. I don't get it," she says.

"Here ya go, hun," Gretchen, the flight attendant, says handing me a plastic container with what I assume is my meal. "I was able to find you a chicken dish after all."

"Thanks, I really appreciate that very much," I say.

"Oh, I almost forgot your wine," she says, handing me a mini bottle of Pinot Grigio. The one problem with this virus-protection thing has been an increase in plastic use. So much for protecting the planet.

"Thanks, again."

She gives me a little wink through the face shield and says, "Anytime sweetie."

Mae gets the text from Nigel during the flight to Austin. She is sitting about three rows back and can't see him, but she does see the flight attendant.

Mae relishes the chance to get out of San Diego. She isn't much of a beach girl, and there isn't much culture in and around San Diego itself. It still kind of has that beachy vibe from the 1960's, and being from San Francisco, Mae likes a little more culture and glitz.

Looking down at her phone, Mae reads the text from Nigel again:

```
One firm contact - blonde stewardess, name
tag says Gretchen, 90% confidence

One soft contact - first class cabin, older
gentleman, black suit, short haircut, big
ears, 15% confidence
```

Mae smiles. She checks out the flight attendant when she comes by with the food. It is always fun trying to figure out who is not in the Face Value database. If Nigel ranked the stewardess at a 90% confidence level, then it is certain that this Gretchen is in their database.

But just to make sure, Mae will take a photograph of Gretchen and upload it into their system. By the time they land, the Face Value software system will have run Gretchen's image against the 300 million images in the database.

The older gentlemen will be another story. If Nigel scored him with a 15% confidence rank, it probably means that his facial characteristics are not found within their database, and that is of concern. So, it is imperative that she gets some kind of photograph of him. Mae will need to get one at the airport, and that is going to be tricky.

PART ONE

CHAPTER 1

Austin-Bergstrom International Airport
Austin, Texas
March 12, 2021

Looking out the airplane window as we taxi to our gate got me thinking. I feel lucky to have the new job with Face Value Corporation. I am excited to attend the 2021 South by Southwest Festival even though it is going to be smaller than in years past.

I have been out of full-time work for about a decade and only working part-time. So, it feels good to be productive and useful. As for the job itself, I just sort of fell into it. I don't know how to write computer code, and I'm not a first responder, but I do have a knack for remembering faces–a knack that sometimes gets me into trouble.

"Come on, Nigel," Clare says. "Get a move on. We need to catch the shuttle to the hotel because the next one won't be for another hour."

Clare and I are stumbling along with the crowd towards baggage claim. Amazingly, people are still wearing all types of face covers and some with gloves even with the relaxed Federal guidelines.

Clare rushes off hoping to claim our bags before I arrive. Suddenly, an image on the right of me comes into focus. The guy from first class. He is standing right next to me, but now he is wearing an N95 face mask. *Christ, just what I need.*

Tall, fit, and trim. Nice suit and a briefcase. Ears are often a give-away. This guy's ears are huge. I don't mean Dumbo huge, but bigger than most. People don't think ears are that different, but they are. And, given the current situation with face masks they have become even more critical for face recognition surveillance.

"Excuse me," I say looking for some point of reference. "Did you hear which baggage carousel for the flight out of San Diego?"

He shakes his head sideways and, in a muffled, Texas drawl says, "Sonny, sure as fire, the bags will be on Carousel 5."

"Uh, pardon me?" I don't quite understand what the fuck "sure as fire" means.

He laughs in that big Texan way and steps in front of me and moves to the left side of the escalator. "Follow me."

We scurry down the final few steps of the escalator and turn right towards what I assume is Carousel 5.

Five minutes later, we arrive at the carousel, and Clare is standing there with our bags.

"Let's go slowpoke," she says still wearing her face cover, quizzing me with her eyes about the Texas guy.

I want to tell Clare that I need more time to identify his face. So, I say, "This guy was helping me find the carousel."

He nods at Clare in that Texas Ranger kind of way. "Howdy, ma'am. Glad to be of service."

He looks over her shoulder towards the carousel and then steps to pick up his bag. Before I can get one final look, he is off. Crap! I need to remember a few details–big ears, fit and trim, wide eyes with brown shades. Short military haircut.

"Watch where you're goin', little lady," I hear the Texas guy say. I look back hoping to get one more look, but I see him rush off, pushing a small Asian woman with a Hello Kitty face cover out of the way.

I take a second look and shake my head. Clare is pulling me along towards the exit. "Let's get to the shuttle, Nigel."

As we push our way onto the airport shuttle, I am reminded how quickly life can change. One short year ago I desperately needed to find a job, and I was a bit agitated with my lack of progress. But now I'm being paid to attend the fancy South by Southwest Festival with a beautiful woman by my side. Who would've thought?

By the time Mae gets to Carousel 5, she sees the older guy chatting with Nigel and Clare. She tries to maneuver inconspicuously to hear the conversation but without much luck. There aren't many people around for her to hide behind.

Mae isn't a big fan of Clare and wonders what Nigel sees in her. She is pretty and does have big boobs, but there is something about her that does not sit right with Mae.

The old guy reaches around Clare to grab his bag off the carousel. This is the opportunity that Mae is looking for. She judges his path and walks in a straight line.

Bump.

"Watch where you're goin', little lady," old guy says to her through his face mask.

Mae pretends to be looking at her phone, "Sorry, sir." Giggling like a schoolgirl through her *Hello Kitty* face cover.

Smile bastard. You're on candid camera. Snap.

With that, Mae moves away, centering the picture of the old guy in the Face Value mobile app. His eyes and ears are prominent in the photograph, which will be helpful for processing. However, even the most robust face recognition software has difficulties identifying faces with such limited biometrics. She had already experienced a few false positives from other pictures taken of people wearing face masks, and the end result was not pretty.

Hitting send, Mae looks back to see Nigel and Clare laughing as they walk off. How cute, Mae thinks. Once she figures out what is going on with the old guy, it is time to learn a little more about *Clare*.

CHAPTER 2

Austin, Texas
March 12, 2021

Before getting on the hotel shuttle, the driver scans Clare and I to make sure we do not have a high temperature. We have to show our 'immunity passport' from the TSA mobile app, which verifies that we have been tested for the coronavirus and are not considered infectious. Then, we have to sanitize our hands because we are not wearing gloves.

After getting on the shuttle and finding a seat, I look around at our fellow passengers. Most are wearing some kind of face protection and gloves, but there are a few like me going rogue. One guy is trying to make small talk with a hot looking redhead and not doing a particularly good job of it. I think his confederate flag bandana might be the problem.

The shuttle pulls up in front of the Austin Hilton. There is a line of people waiting to board, dreading the 30-minute pre-boarding process. Clare and I disembark. I pick up our bags and stumble down the small stairway.

"Nigel, give the man a tip," Clare bellows as she heads into the hotel. I fumble through my pockets, hoping to find something. I pull out a few dollars and a piece of gum.

The shuttle driver looks at my offering over his face mask and shakes his head, "Don't worry, man. Who wants to touch cash anymore?" But he does take the piece of gum with gloved hands. "Juicy Fruit. I love this stuff, reminds me of growing up," he remarks, turning to climb back into the shuttle bus.

The Austin Hilton isn't one of the new trendy hotels, but it has recently been renovated to comply with the new Federal Social Distance guidelines. Located almost adjacent to the Austin Convention Center, it offers access to almost all the venues being held at SXSW.

I walk up to the front desk just as the attendant spoke to Clare, "Thanks for providing your immunity passport and face scan. We have you registered for one of our executive suites with a king-size bed. I just need a credit card," the slightly frumpy looking man says through his custom face shield.

People have been using the clear panel shields instead of a face mask in preparation for new Federal regulations. There is legislation pending Senate approval mandating a clear line of sight for a person's mouth to help protect the rights of the hearing impaired and seniors who rely upon lip reading.

Face masks were the obvious choice at the beginning of the coronavirus outbreak, but issues with those with glasses and a feeling of suffocation prompted the need for alternatives. The face shield seems to be catching on because it provides a full view of a person's face and doesn't make one feel like they are in the hospital.

I look around to check out the lobby. I can see staff and guests wearing a variety of face coverings although the face mask is still the most common type. I don't see any faces that catch my attention, but I notice that the concierge is good looking, even with her custom face mask on.

"Nigel, give the man your credit card," barks Clare through the Prada shawl draped across her face. She likes this more stylish look than a face mask. And, truthfully, I like it much better as well.

"Sorry, I was just checking out the lobby. Very nice," I say handing over my American Express card to the attendant who grabs it with gloved fingers.

"Why thank you, Mr. Grant. And thank you for being a gold Hilton Rewards member. We are immensely proud of our hotel and restaurant. Make sure you check with concierge services about the many events in town this weekend. South by Southwest takes over a lot of venues, but with a smaller festival this year there are some other attractions that you might find of interest."

"Yes, I think I will come down later and see what's going on," giving the attendant a friendly smile.

"Okay, your room is on the 10th floor on our Executive Level. There is a separate lounge up there with fresh fruit all day long and a wine reception at 6 PM," the front desk attendant says. "And, rest assured that we take great care keeping our facility clean and sterile as per Federal regulations. Our housekeeping staff disinfects the elevators and escalators every hour." He hands me the little envelope with the digital key. "Do you need help with your luggage?" he asks looking down at our bags.

"Nope, got that covered, but thanks," I say reaching down to pick up the bags.

Clare and I head over to the bank of elevators. Clare turns to me, "So, you're going to check in with the concierge to see what's going on in town, are you?" she bristles. "It wouldn't have anything to do with that tight skirt she's wearing, would it?"

"You know, I didn't even notice that," turning to look at the young lady. "Why gosh, you're correct. She does fill out that skirt."

Clare punches me in the arm. "You're such a liar, Nigel. Go on, have your fun with her," she teases, "But, first you might want to see what I have planned for tonight!"

Clare and I are excited to travel after having been locked down in San Diego, and we are thankful that some of the restrictions have been lifted. The Federal travel guidelines allow individuals the choice to wear face coverings and gloves. However, it is still mandated that any business that offers client-facing services must provide face protection to their employees when requested. It also shortens the social distance requirement to arm length. However, one new little twist that is causing a lot of headaches requires that every individual has to be subjected to a thermal face scan when traveling on public transportation and attending events of 50 or more or public venues like restaurants and bars.

The ACLU and other privacy groups are up in arms about the impact of these travel guidelines on personal freedom. Protecting the citizen from harm is all that matters in today's world. The loss of privacy and freedom is sweeping the world, agnostic of the government affiliation.

I don't really give a damn. I figure that when my time is up, there isn't much I can do. Wearing a mask and washing my hands isn't going to get me through the pearly gates anyway. I lost that opportunity years ago!

Riding up the elevator to our room, Clare continues to tease me about the concierge. Thankfully, as soon as the door opens on our floor, she races out of the elevator to get to our room. She places the digital key on the sensor and pushes the door open, not thinking about holding the door for me. I catch the door with one of the bags and then slip through before it closes.

"Stop, don't go any further, buster," she commands, camera at the ready.

Oh, brother, here we go again–the ritual. Clare starts taking pictures of the room: how it looks from the door, what the bathroom looks like, and how the amenities are laid out.

"That is quite the view," I comment, hoping to direct her attention away from the door.

I would kind of like to put this bag down.

"Just a second. I've got to take a picture of the beds. Look how they have those nice chocolates laid out with a welcome card," she says.

For the moment, I am glad that her attention is focused on picture taking. I've got to put these bags down and go visit the john. Traveling wreaks havoc on my daily constitutional.

"Clare. Do you need to use the bathroom?" I ask, placing the bags on the floor.

"No, go ahead, but turn on that fan. I don't want you stinking up the room," Clare says.

But, before I get to make the move, a bell chimes. "Clare, your phone is buzzing."

"It isn't my phone. It's the door-bell," she replies, lowering the Prada shawl to her shoulders.

Being one for safety, I look through the peephole at a figure that takes up the whole field of vision. Wow, that is one big dude.

"Hello? Who is it?" I say in my deepest voice.

"Hotel Security, Mr. Grant."

I open the door slowly, peering through the crack.

"Sorry to bother you, Mr. Grant. But it appears we did not get your thermal scan. Can you come down to the front desk?" asks the security guy through his face mask. He is wearing a traditional face mask with a swirly Hilton logo placed front and center on the mask. It looks a bit odd on his gigantic head.

This guy is about 6'6" and the size of a small rhino. "You play at UT?" I joke, my voice wobbling.

"Nope, Baylor. Can we get you down to the front desk now, Mr. Grant!" he says with a little bit of urgency.

"Yeah, let me get a few things unpacked, and I will be right down. Is that okay?" I say dismissively.

"No problem, I will just wait out here for you," Security Guy says firmly.

Okay, have it your way, but I gotta take that dump, and then I will go down to the front desk.

"What is that all about?" asks Clare, looking up from her phone sans face cover.

"They forgot to do the thermal scan," I reply.

"I wondered why they didn't do that," she says.

About 20 minutes later, I step out of my hotel room, expecting Security Guy to have gotten bored and moved on.

"Everything okay?" he says looking at me from across the hallway. His massive body is covering up the door across the hall.

"Yep, just had to make a little pit stop," I say, realizing that I have forgotten my mask.

He nods his head with understanding. He speaks into a microphone on his sleeve, like the secret service.

"I'm coming down with Mr. Grant."

As I watch him lumber down the hallway, with a decided limp on the right side, I am reminded of my friend, Carle. He has a bum right knee.

"You play O-line?" I ask.

"Yes, sir. Strong side, right tackle. I played all four years at Baylor. We went to the Cotton Bowl my senior year, which is what got me to the 'Boys," he strides through the hallway on a mission. Deliver Mr. Grant to the front desk.

Security Guy and I exit the elevator, our casual chat about football and Baylor over. I felt small and frail standing next to him in the elevator, which is something, because I'm no slouch. I am about 6'2" on a good day albeit about twenty pounds overweight.

"Mr. Grant."

I find myself standing at the front desk with some manager dude looking at me over a Hilton-logo face shield.

"Mr. Grant. Are you okay?" he quizzes me.

Damn, why do people always think something is wrong with me? "Yes, I'm great. Thanks," I respond with as much assurance as I can. "What a great hotel you have here. Our room is magnificent."

"And, he said the bathroom facilities are top-notch," says Security Guy, conveying in a sly way why we were running late.

"Yes, sorry for the delay, but travel upsets my stomach," I say looking at Security Guy. *Screw you. Hope you get arthritis in that bum knee of yours, asshole.*

"No problem. Travel does take its toll on the old digestive system. Make sure you hydrate. That is what I find most beneficial," Manager Dude comments in that all-knowing way.

"That will be enough, Dwight. There appears to be a problem up on the 4th floor. Go check it out and report back."

Dwight! Never would've guessed that one. He seems more of the generation that named their boys Josh or Kyle, maybe even, Cody. Trendy names. Not Dwight.

"Nice chatting with you, Dwight," I chime in my most annoying voice. Dwight turns around and gives me what I assume is a 'just you wait, fucker' look.

Manager Dude watches Dwight lumber off to the 4th floor. "Dwight means well. He doesn't have the best interpersonal skills," Manager Dude comments. "I think it might have something to do with his head getting banged around in his helmet."

We watch Dwight walk into the elevator. His massive body filling every nook and cranny.

"Yep, correct on all accounts," I say. "Now I guess you need to scan my face?"

"Say, cheese!" the manager dude says. "Thank you very much, Mr. Grant. I also need to see your TSA immunity passport?"

"No problem," I say placing my phone on the counter. "Here you go."

It is pretty simple and quick. They have one of the newer FLIR systems with the digital camera and thermal detector all in one. It is the state of art and offers the best resolution for face recognition in the industry.

The fact that it does more than just assess your temperature is often overlooked by most people. I suspect the media doesn't know, and the government doesn't really want that detail to be common knowledge.

"So, where do you guys store all of this data?" I ask.

"Oh, we don't store anything," says the manager dude. "We just verify that you don't have a fever and then check your facial image with the Federal database. If everything checks out, it gets purged from our system every night."

I look at him, realizing that he doesn't know shit about what is going on, so I just say, "Uh huh" and go back to my room.

What he doesn't know is that there is about 10% of the population not in that Federal database, and when extrapolated worldwide the figure climbs to about 15%. The problem is determining whether those individuals aren't in there because of some hiccup in the system or because they are actively working to not get discovered.

As I step out of the elevator, I am reminded that without all of these concerns regarding face recognition, I wouldn't have this wonderful new career.

I come back to the room in good spirits and a smile. "What's with the smile?" asks Clare, walking towards me with a mischievous grin.

"Oh, nothing. I was just thinking about how lucky I am that the world needs help identifying people in real time," I comment.

"How so? Clare asks.

"Well, for one I wouldn't have this wonderful job," I say pulling her close, "and two, I wouldn't have had the pleasure of meeting you."

"Who, me? Or, do you mean the concierge?" she says, running her hand down along my thigh.

"Nope. Not even tempted," I say proudly. Actually, I did look over at the concierge desk, but the cute blonde was gone, so I just came back to the room.

"What are the plans for tonight?" I ask.

"I don't know, let's go see what downtown Austin has to offer," Clare replies, brushing her breasts across my face, "and then we can discuss dessert when we come back."

Austin, Texas – a town renowned for its barbeque, and all I can think about is dessert.

PART TWO

CHAPTER 3

San Diego, California
Monday, December 21, 2020

The spring term at Portland State didn't start until January 4th, so I decided to head down to San Diego for some sunshine over Christmas break. I figured the warmer weather would do me good and improve my tan. Besides, I was in desperate need to travel and get out of Portland. With the coronavirus outbreak early in the year, I hadn't had a chance to do any of my normal summer travel. In fact, my three-week trip to Italy and France was cancelled because of limits on foreign travelers into those countries.

There was still time before boarding the plane to San Diego, so I headed over to get some coffee at the Starbucks kiosk near my gate. It is one of the few vendors that survived the coronavirus pandemic. Most of the restaurants and shops closed and never returned. The whole travel experience is different. People just wander aimlessly before boarding their flights. Who wants to be stuck near a bunch of possible virus vectors?

Walking towards the Starbucks near the gate for my flight, I saw a poster located at the entrance of the moving walkway.

There were a bunch of different faces splattered around on the poster with some text that said, "Do you remember faces?"

Yeah, I'm fairly good at remembering faces, I thought.

The faces on the poster were of different shapes, sizes, and ethnicities. In addition, they were in different positions with a lot of text and scribble mixed in. And, some of them showed people with face masks or sunglasses and ball caps. At the bottom in bold letters it said, "Interested in a job? Want to live in San Diego?"

Yeah, I want a job, and who wouldn't want to live in fucking San Diego?

There was a contact phone number at the bottom of the poster. Since I was going down to San Diego, I thought, *what the heck*. They hadn't started to board the plane yet, so I called the number on the poster. It rang through, and I was transferred to their Human Resources department. A nice sounding babe took the call and told me they were booked for today, but that I was welcome to meet with the HR manager tomorrow, Tuesday, at 10 AM.

The next morning, I took a short ride over to the office in Sorrento Valley, which is technically Mira Mesa and not San Diego, but let's not get picky. I arrived at my appointed time and was marched into an office on the first floor. It wasn't much of an office, just a desk, with some folders laying on the desk and a filing cabinet in the back. It looked pretty spartan and clean. The desk had a plexiglass panel running down the middle, separating the interviewer and the interviewee.

About 20 minutes later, in walked a very tall, nice looking woman about my age. She sat across from me in a plain, black suit, white blouse, and simple white pearls. No mask. No gloves. Interesting.

"Your name, please?" she asked, peering at me through the clear plexiglass panel.

"Nigel Grant."

"Your age?"

"Do I have to share that?"

"Yes, you do," she smiled.

"50," I provided.

"When?"

"When what?" I questioned.

Pretty Lady stared; her eyes fixed on me. "When is your birthday?" she said slowly.

"Octoooober 21st, 1970," I said slowly back.

She gave me a quirky grin and then smiled. "Okay," she scribbled something on the form on the desk.

Pretty Lady looked at me, slowly twisting those white pearls around her finger. "My name is Bernadette by the way."

"Okay, now that we're on a first name basis," I said, "What now?"

"What made you apply for this job?"

"I saw the advertisement at the Portland airport yesterday. It seemed interesting. Is this part of Homeland Security?" I asked.

She looked at me as if she were sizing me up. "No, it is not part of Homeland Security, and there is no direct connection with the government. This is a private company position," she said rather firmly.

"What part of interesting, do you mean?" she queried, waiting for my response.

"Come again? I don't quite follow," I said.

"Well, you said you saw the advertisement, and it seemed interesting. What was it that seemed interesting?" Bernadette asked.

She pushed a piece of paper across the table. It is the advertisement with the faces from the airport. I stared at it, thinking, *Hmm, what did I find interesting then?* My mind began to wander. *Is there a correct answer to her question?*

She was extremely attractive. I looked around the office trying to waste time.

"Mr. Grant. Can we focus here!" she asked.

"How come you're not wearing a mask?" I asked.

"I don't think it's necessary."

"Okay, I agree," I said. "What was your question?"

"What did you find interesting about the advertisement at the airport?" she said in an exasperated tone.

I looked at her. "Well, the title on the poster said, 'Do you remember faces?', which I thought was quite interesting. And, then all those pictures of different faces including the ones with face masks got my attention."

"Yes. And, did any of those faces seem familiar?" she asked, leaning in.

My mind immediately jumped to the one face that stood out. It was of a movie star, Bradley something. He did that movie with Lady Gaga. Brad Pitt, something. No, he doesn't go by *Bradley.*

Pretty Lady looked irritated but sensed some trepidation on my part. "Mr. Grant, it's okay. You don't have to share that information. Many of our candidates see faces that seem familiar, but they are afraid to mention it." She checked off some boxes on the form and looked at me. "What is your academic background?"

"Well, I did undergraduate at Cal State Northridge," I said, thinking about my time in the San Fernando Valley.

"What was your major?" she asked.

"I majored in business at Cal State Northridge. I was thinking of becoming an attorney. But, after working at a law firm in Los Angeles for a couple of years, I realized that the legal profession wasn't for me."

"Okay, and after Northridge?" Bernadette asked.

"Well, about 10 years later, I went to Boston University for my MBA. They had a great business school, and I always wanted to live in Boston," I answered remembering a favorite song,

Please come to Boston for the springtime.

I'm staying here with some friends and they've got lots of room.

You can sell your paintings on the sidewalk, by a café where I hope to be working soon.

Please come to Boston, she said no. Would you come home to me. And she said.

Hey, rambling boy, why don't you settle down.

Was that by Kenny Loggins or Dave Loggins? I always get them confused.

"Mr. Grant, please let's focus!" she said. "What year did you start your MBA in Boston?"

I looked at her. She had that annoyed look, the one that Jennifer, my ex-wife, gave me when she felt I was daydreaming.

"Let's see, that would have been around...2000 or 2001," I guessed.

"Which is it?" she asked.

"It was 2000," I said firmly. "I finished my MBA in 2002 and hooked up with an investment banking firm, where I spent seven years in their mergers and acquisitions group before the Great Recession of 2009."

Bernadette fumbled around for a bit. Seemingly irritated about something. Then, her phone rang.

"Yes. Uh, huh," she said. "I understand." Placing the phone down, Pretty Lady looked up and smiled.

"Let's take a break. I was hoping to get some more background information on you, but it won't be available until a little later," Bernadette said, kind of disappointed.

I got the feeling she was hoping for information that she could use to send me packing.

"Can you come back in about 30 minutes or so?" she requested. "Get yourself some coffee downstairs in our cafeteria."

"No problem," I said walking out the door.

I got some coffee at the barista coffee station and walked around the lobby. It was an impressive office building with a lot of people buzzing around. Some were wearing face masks, and some were not. But they all seemed quite animated and busy.

I was thinking this had to be the craziest job interview I'd ever had when I was startled out of my thought.

"Mr. Grant," Bernadette said coming up from behind me. "Thanks for waiting. I hope you enjoyed your coffee."

"Yes, I had a great time relaxing and enjoying the view," I commented. "If this is what it's like every day, then sign me up."

Bernadette smiled. "Well, let's not get ahead of ourselves."

Boom. Punch to the stomach.

"How long did you say you've been out of work?" Bernadette asked, as we walked back towards the interview room. She had her glasses on and, quite frankly, looked sexy as hell. "After you, please," she said holding the door open.

"Now, you were saying?" Bernadette asked sitting down behind the desk.

"Saying what?" I questioned.

"How long you have you been out of full-time work."

"Oh, yeah. Since about 2015, although I've had a few part-time positions since then. Now most of the time I teach part-time in the business school at Portland State University," I sighed. "It has been hard finding full time work because of my age."

Bernadette gave me a courteous smile and said, "We don't discriminate on age. In fact, we find that older workers tend to have better aptitude for staying on task and using their long-term memory."

"That's great news," I said. Not sure I liked falling under the 'older worker' category.

"Well, let's try to finish this up. I'm going to have you look at some pictures," she said. "Let me know if you recognize any of them or notice anything about them."

With that she slid a color print of a woman in front of me. "Have you ever seen this woman?"

I took a good, long look. *Nice looking babe, but* "No."

"How about this one?"

"Nope, although the relationship between her eyes and the bridge of the nose seems familiar."

"This one?"

"Maybe. He has a pretty standard face, strong chin, and broad cheek bones."

And, just when I thought we were done, she slid over a picture of a good-looking blonde with short hair, green eyes, and wearing a face covering.

"Umm, yeah. I've seen her," I said.

"How about this one?"

"Yep," *older guy, beard, crooked nose with big ears.*

"And, this one?"

I took a long look at the picture. The face had soft, feminine characteristics although the person wore a floppy hat and big sunglasses.

Long pause, *these people seem awfully familiar to me.* "Yes, I remember her."

"Nigel, I want you to think really hard. Where have you seen the people in these photographs?" Bernadette asked.

I thought about the faces and wandered around in my brain, trying to figure out where I had seen those people. *High school? No.*

College? No, but maybe...that blonde looked like the sorority girl I banged on the beach at a spring break party in Cabo.

The guy with the crooked nose. He did look familiar. Was it from the investment firm? I am trying hard to remember.

"Nigel?" Bernadette said.

"Give me a second. I am thinking about it." Then, it slowly dawned on me.

"I remember them from the poster at the airport," I said.

Bernadette let out a sigh, almost like she had been holding her breath. "Phew. Well done, Mr. Grant. I was beginning to think that this position wasn't for you."

She picked up her phone and punched in some numbers. "Any luck?" she said into the mouth receiver.

"Really? That's what you said a couple of hours ago." Bernadette looked at me from across the desk. The phone still cradled next to her ear. "Okay," slamming the phone on the cradle.

"We would like for you to come back tomorrow morning, say 10?" she asked.

"Sure, I can come back. Any recommendations for drinks or dinner?" I said suggestively.

"There is a taxi out front waiting to take you back to your hotel," Bernadette replied. "Have a good night."

CHAPTER 4

Face Value Headquarters
San Diego, California
Wednesday, December 22, 2020

I was sitting in that same small room from yesterday. I was a bit fuzzy from way too many drinks and not enough sleep from the night before. And, it was way too early to be meeting with Bernadette who stared at me through the plexiglass.

Her arms folded, she inquired, "Well, did you have a good time last night?"

"As a matter of fact, I did," I yawned. "That Gaslamp Quarter is a pretty crazy place."

"I wouldn't know," Bernadette said a bit perturbed.

"Now as I said yesterday, Nigel, we do a good job of vetting all our candidates," she said off-handedly. "Quite frankly, most of our candidates never make it to this stage."

She looked down at her notes and then pulled out a blue folder.

"When did you prepare this report on Black Matte Laboratories?" she asked.

I stared straight ahead, looking at the folder, wondering how in the hell she got access to that report. It was one of my last projects when I worked at the Los Angeles law firm. It was information I had pulled together for our litigation team on the Lakewood High School case. A case that garnered national headlines and disdain around the world.

"Umm, how did you get that report?" I stammered.

"I have my sources, Nigel. We do a thorough job of vetting all our candidates," she reiterated. "And, I must say this report has some interesting information related to face recognition," she said leaning back in her chair, crossing her arms.

Yeah, but that still didn't answer my question about how she got that file. That case had top secret clearance stamped on every page. "Lucky me," I said worriedly, "it's just that the project related to Black Matte is classified."

Bernadette leaned over her desk. She was wearing a blue blazer with an off-white tank underneath and some really tight jeans. "Nigel, trust me. We know everything about our candidates," she said somewhat flirtatiously.

Um, that sounded a bit worrisome.

"Now let's chat a little about Black Matte Laboratories," Bernadette said. "How did they go from being non-existent to managing a multi-million-dollar project for Draper Laboratories?"

"Pretty simple. They were a small company based outside of Boston in the late 1960's, contracted by the Massachusetts Institute of Technology to continue investigation of heat properties of reflective coatings for use on surface structures." I continued, "They had rights to an obscure patent from the early days of the Material Sciences Division out of DARPA that was developed in support of Project Rainbow."

"What was Project Rainbow?" Bernadette asked.

"It was the code name for a project funded by the Central Intelligence Agency in the late 1950's to determine the feasibility of reducing radar cross-section identification," I offered. "It was an early attempt to determine the feasibility of changing the radar signature through structural design."

"And, how did MIT get involved?" she queried.

"Well, by the mid 1960's Project Rainbow was considered a failure, and most of the proposed ideas were proven inadequate," I mentioned. "Dr. Charles Draper, was an aeronautical engineer, who managed the MIT Instrumentation Laboratory. He was tasked with determining if there were any viable projects from the information collected from Project Rainbow. One of the projects focused on a new composite material that could reduce the heat signature from jet engines. The lead engineer needed help understanding this new composite material..."

"And?" Bernadette asked looking at me through the plexiglass.

"Um," I coughed, feeling a little uncomfortable that I wasn't wearing a face mask. "It was quite serendipitous that one of the Black Matte employees had spent some time in England on sabbatical. He was in the laboratory where they identified a rudimentary way to isolate single layers of graphite, a material known today as graphene."

Bernadette looked at me. I was wondering whether she understood any of this. Quite frankly, I barely understood it.

"Okay, so how does Project Rainbow come into play with stealth technology?" Bernadette queried.

I froze. "I don't know what you're talking about," I remarked, hoping to move past that question.

"Come on, Nigel. I know about the work on stealth technology funded by Project Rainbow out of DARPA," she shared.

I looked around the room for any hidden cameras or microphones. This line of questioning was getting deep into the woods about my work at the law firm.

"Um, let's suppose I know something about this 'stealth technology.' It is possible that it was instrumental in the design of an aircraft structure that could evade radar detection through an innovative design," I nodded. Comfortable that this answer wouldn't get me into too much trouble.

Bernadette looked over at me with a big smile leaning towards me…whispering, "And, would that aircraft be the F-117 Nighthawk?"

Shit. How does she know this stuff?!

"Nigel, tell me how Black Matte Laboratories and Project Rainbow fit into the F-117 program?" she questioned.

"Well, you have to understand the position of the United States intelligence community after World War II," I instructed. "They knew that the Russians were up to something, but it was very difficult to get much information out of the Soviet Union in those days."

"The launch of the Sputnik satellite by the Russians in 1957 caught the United States intelligence community completely by surprise."

I continued, "And the CIA vowed never to be in that position again. So, a joint project with the Department of Defense decided the best plan would be to fly over the Soviet Union and take pictures. It was a good plan, a simple plan. They enlisted Lockheed to build the U-2 spy plane and Dr. Edward Land to build a camera that could capture the smallest detail on the ground."

I yawned, feeling the lack of sleep and food on my brain function. "But…"

"Okay, but what?" Bernadette said, inching towards the end of her chair.

"Well, they didn't count on how advanced the Russian missile technology had become," I said. "The U-2 plane developed by Lockheed Corporation in the late 1950's was conceived as more of a long-range, high-altitude glider than a jet. It was meant to glide above the known altitude that was considered achievable by Russian jet fighters and higher than current Russian surface-to-air missile capability."

I looked at my watch, wondering how much longer this interview would last.

"Sadly, for the pilot, Gary Powers, the Soviet missile technology had advanced far enough to reach him gliding some 70,000 feet above the Ural Mountains," I commented. "He survived the direct hit by a Russian missile but was captured by local peasants and held by the Soviet government."

"Nigel, I appreciate the history lesson, but where does Black Matte come into play?" Bernadette said.

"Well, you asked about Project Rainbow, and the only way to understand it, is the back story," I said firmly.

"Okay but try and speed it up," she remarked looking at her watch.

I wondered what this had to do with my interview but continued,

"Well, the ever-crafty US intelligence community learned that higher did not necessarily mean better, so they came up with the brilliant idea of higher and faster for surveillance purposes. This new program began in the late 1950's, resulting in the development of perhaps one of the most highly engineered airplanes in history—the SR71, or the Blackbird. The Blackbird entered official service in 1967 and was instrumental in some of the greatest reconnaissance missions of all time."

"Nigel," Bernadette smiled. "Let's focus and get this over with."

"Ultimately, the Blackbirds were retired in 1999," I said, realizing that I was getting hungry, but I continued,

"The U-2 and Blackbird surveillance programs generated a tremendous amount of information on materials science, software design and function, guidance systems, and engine technology, but it was becoming noticeably clear that standard aeronautical engineering had a limited lifetime.

"Thankfully, a research fellow out of Black Matte revisited some of the early work from Project Rainbow. Her idea was revolutionary but considered impossible. Instead of using traditional aerodynamic design theory, she proposed that a plane, the F-117, be built based on its radar cross-sectional area and not traditional aerodynamics."

She leaned forward in her chair. "And?"

I added,

"Well, this concept had never been considered. Basically, the surface of the aircraft would consist of non-aerodynamic, geometric planes rather than the sleek lines traditionally used in jet aircraft.

"It was proposed that for the F-117, the surface of the plane would consist of these geometric planes in a variety of configurations. You know, triangles, rhomboids, rectangles... This would limit the aerodynamics of the aircraft for flight, but it was hoped that it would reflect radar away, making it invisible."

I paused, waiting to see Bernadette's reaction. "Oh, my God, Nigel! Where does Black Matte fit into this?"

"Well, Black Matte had access to an advanced software program out of Carnegie Mellon University that was capable of analyzing a tremendous amount of data," I said. "They were one of the leading academic computer science centers at the time with their early work on artificial intelligence and computational analysis."

"What did you learn about the Carnegie Mellon system?" asked Bernadette a bit exasperated.

"Well, the purpose of their system was to help analyze all of the information from the simulation models being collected on the various designs," I admitted. "It seemed that the speed of the Carnegie Mellon system allowed for a very robust learning environment in order to identify the best arrangement for the geometric surface planes."

"But, I'm not really sure," I apologized.

Bernadette stood up, coming around the desk and breaking the social distance rule, and said directly to my face, "And, why aren't you sure?"

"I'm not sure because anything related to Black Matte Technologies and the Lakewood High School case was deemed a national security matter in 1993."

"Really?" she said quite loudly, leaning in towards me.

I sat back in my chair, afraid of the closeness but at the same time wanting to lean in and give her a kiss.

"Yes, really! Now, what does this have to do with my job application?" I yelled back.

CHAPTER 5

The frustration between me and Bernadette about Black Matte Technologies was quite evident when a good-looking babe nervously opened the door to the room. "Everything okay in here?" she asked peering over her stylish face covering.

"It's okay, Clare," Bernadette said. "Mr. Grant and I were just finishing up."

Quite frankly, I didn't know if I could take more of her questioning, so I was pleased when she said, 'finishing up.' Hopefully, that meant I would soon be out by the pool at the hotel. Something that I hadn't been able to do with all this interviewing.

"Sorry about that heated exchange, Nigel," Bernadette said. "The Black Matte project has some pretty significant relevance to our work here at Face Value."

I didn't really have a clue what she was talking about and didn't really care. I was ready to move on from the interview and get back to the hotel.

Bernadette jotted down a few notes on the uptake form and

stood up and came around the desk. I stood up thinking she was going to send me along my way.

"Thank you for the interview," I said, ready to make my exit. "I appreciate your consideration."

Bernadette looked at me, "Congratulations, Mr. Grant. I am honored to offer you a job as an authenticator with Face Value."

I stood there for a few minutes. Trying to figure out if I heard her correctly.

"Everything okay? Mr. Grant?" she queried.

I wavered a bit, holding onto the back of the chair for support. "Thank you. I don't know quite what to say. I sure didn't expect this when I called from Portland and surely not after our little chat about Black Matte Technologies."

Bernadette came back around her desk. The smell of her perfume still strong and inviting. *Jo Malone, perhaps?* Lightly floral with a hint of cinnamon and vanilla. I didn't know if we should fist bump or shake hands to close the deal.

"No problem. Like I said, we like to know all that we can about our candidates. And, if that means putting them in the pressure-cooker, so be it," she said with a grin while motioning a high five.

"Well, you sure did put a little heat on the fire," I said, raising my hand in the air to reciprocate.

"Then I did my job. Now let's get you over to human resources. They will discuss your benefits and review some company policies," Bernadette said.

She lightly grabbed my elbow and turned me towards the door. "Professor Gallegos will answer any questions you might have during the onboarding process. He likes to meet all of our new authenticators and fill them in on the backstory."

Authenticator. She said it again. That is a strange job title.

"Nigel, right this way," Bernadette was standing in front of Human Resources. "Let's get you acquainted with Greta. She will take it from here."

I was still stuck on authenticator and wondering what skill I had that fell under that category.

"Nigel," Bernadette said, pulling me through the door and into the Human Resources office. "Meet Greta."

"Greta, I want you to meet Mr. Grant," she said.

Greta stood before me, a blonde Nordic goddess. I stood there mesmerized. Stammering like an idiot!

"Nigel, sit down," Bernadette pushed me towards the chair.

"Hello, Mr. Grant. Just take a seat right there, and I will pull your employment record up on my computer and we can get started," Greta commanded.

"Greta, when you are done with Mr. Grant, please direct him down to the cafeteria," Bernadette said. "I want to introduce Nigel to our cafeteria staff."

"Sure thing, Bernie," Greta said, focused more on the paperwork in front of her. Long blonde hair, perfectly manicured nails. Dressed to the nines and sporting what looked like a Chanel face covering.

I tried to think of something to say, but I couldn't. My mind had gone blank. Slowly I looked around, looking for photographs of a husband, kids, a dog. Anything for some chit-chat. But, nothing. Greta was tied to her job.

"Okay, Mr. Grant," Greta said peering over her face cover. I could make out the subtle Chanel logo that blended with the Chanel name sewn throughout the fabric.

"Call me, Nigel," I said.

"Okay. Nigel, it is," she said looking at her computer monitor and then at me. Her deep blue eyes framed by the contrasting color of her face cover. I could feel them pierce right through me like a laser beam.

"Well, good for you. I see Bernadette coded you as an Authenticator III. Well done! Bernie rarely gives that to new authenticators," those blue eyes looked at me approvingly.

"Level III starts at $100,000 per year with a very nice expense account," Greta said. "You get health insurance, a defined benefit plan, and the option to participate in our stock purchase program."

"Do you have family, Nigel?" Greta asked.

I had just collected my wits from her piercing gaze, and now I was confounded by what I just heard.

Did she say 100,000? And, an expense account with health insurance?

"Nigel?" Greta queried.

"No, I don't. Well, not anymore," I said. *Christ. I hadn't had a salary like that since, well, since the days at the investment banking firm.*

"Your office will be on the third floor. You will have access to our most up-to-date and sophisticated software system for your assignments." Greta slid some forms across the desk.

Did she say office? I was hoping this wasn't all just a dream.

"Did you say, office?" I questioned, feeling somewhat awkward that I wasn't wearing a face cover.

"Yes. Now review these documents, especially the non-disclosure agreement and federal employment guidelines."

"I thought Bernadette said there was no government affiliation?" I said.

"Well, I think she uses a very liberal meaning of affiliation. We are actually a sub-contractor for a large corporation that has a government contract to look at face recognition patterns," Greta confided, looking at me with her beautiful blue eyes.

How in the hell could I say no to this job? Free lunch. Babes galore. And, more money than I had seen in a decade.

"Professor Gallegos will go over the details about our government projects when you meet with him."

Greta slid over more forms. "Just review these documents, sign and date, and I will get you set up for a meeting with the Professor next month," Greta nodded her head approvingly. "Of course, assuming you want the job?"

Are you kidding me? I was 50 years old and broke. Of course, I wanted the job. I needed the job.

"Yes, I would very much like to work here. It sounds wonderful, and I can't wait to meet Professor Gallegos," I reflected, signing the forms before she changed her mind.

"Great. I think you'll enjoy the job. There are a lot of additional benefits," Greta said.

PART THREE

CHAPTER 6

Los Angeles, California
Spring, 1988

When Carle first arrived in Los Angeles to live with his cousin, he didn't really know what to expect. The racial turmoil of the 1960's and 1970's carried over to the mid-1980's. Discontent, fear, and greed all played out in and around the city of Los Angeles.

One thing that was in plenty of commodity was opportunity, from the hip hop artists making a run at the old school rock and roll music producers to the Bloods and the Crips trying to carve out territory in Los Angeles county and throughout Southern California.

There was a feeling in the air that one could do almost anything. And, this was definitely true for his cousin, Wayne, as far as Carle could tell. Cousin Wayne was in a world of his own, a world that Carle did not understand. The movie industry job seemed a little shady for Carle. And, in fact, Wayne seemed a little shady to Carle, as well, which is why he did not take Wayne up on his offer to stay at his crib.

Carle's apartment in Manhattan Beach was perfect. It was right on the beach with easy access to Los Angeles, Santa Monica, and the beaches of Orange County. In fact, Carle was trying to surf, but he was not having much luck, partly because it was difficult, and he still had weakness in his right leg. Another problem he was having was the noticeable racism at most surf spots. He was often pushed off his board by the locals who yelled obscenities laced with bigotry and hatred. Little did they know it just made Carle want to try harder and to show them that surfing wasn't just a white-boy sport.

Separate from the surfing hassles, Carle really enjoyed the area around Manhattan Beach. There were lots of parks for running and Mexican restaurants serving traditional street tacos, not that crap he ate in Atlanta. If the beach made his personal life complete, then his job at TRW filled in the career path bubble.

Carle had been living in Manhattan Beach for a couple of weeks before he decided to venture up to Venice Beach and check out the roller-blading scene that he had read about in the Los Angeles Times Sunday edition. The article said that Venice was the place to be if you wanted to experience all that SoCal had to offer.

Carle drove his 1985 Buick LeSabre up to Venice Beach. Grandpa Harper had given it to him when he graduated from Morehouse. It was the Limited Edition, which seemed to get a lot of attention the few times he had driven it around the area. He soon learned that the size could be problematic when looking for parking at the coastal beach towns.

On the way back from Venice, Carle decided to take a different route back home. He would later think this decision was directed by the hand of God as his father predicted so long ago. Driving south down Aviation Boulevard from LAX he came across the headquarters of TRW, a name that was unfamiliar to him. The hand of God played out as he drove around the immense perimeter of the sprawling buildings, parking lots, and manufacturing facilities.

Carle pulled over on North Douglas Street near the entrance to the massive TRW complex. He was impressed with the mock-up of missiles and jet fighters that were staged for all to see. It showed strength and the American spirit, something that he wanted to experience. As he turned around to head home, perched no more than 50 feet away on a billboard, was the path he had been looking for. It said, TRW is hiring. Positions available in manufacturing and management. College degree preferred."

Carle called the phone number on the billboard the very next day. With a bachelor's degree from Morehouse, the human resources person commented that he sounded perfect for their new management training program and set up an appointment for him later in the week.

Sitting in the lobby of human resources Carle could feel more than see the stares from those coming and going through the main door. It was like they had never seen a person of color before, which he would later learn was more fact than fiction.

As the HR manager told him, since TRW was a government contractor, they were mandated to follow and support all Federal programs on hiring. A recent audit had revealed that they were not in compliance with the 1965 Executive Order 11246 related to affirmative action as it related to minority hiring within the workforce. So, as the manager said without apology, the fact that Carle was Black made it all the better for him to get offered a position in their new management trainee program.

Inside, Carle felt something stir, but he couldn't quite put his finger on it and let it pass. Besides, he was just excited to get hired and work for the company. Earlier that day he had gone to the Redondo Beach library to learn more about the company to prepare for the interview. The chance to help man colonize space was all it took to make him say, "yes."

In retrospect, Carle liked the sense of purpose he had working at TRW, but what he liked most was the history of the company. Every employee got the story during their first week. This is the story:

Simon Ramo and David Wooldridge were electronics engineers affiliated with Hughes Aircraft and the Hughes Electronics division. They were on the leading edge of guided missile technology when they had a little disagreement with Howard Hughes.

Howard Hughes didn't make it easy for them; there were threats, legal challenges, and potential violence. In the end, all parties agreed to separate amicably with the new Ramo-Wooldridge Company earning some Hughes Aircraft contracts. Thompson Products Company, out of Cleveland, Ohio, provided initial funding for the early start-up of Ramo-Wooldridge. Thompson started in 1901 as the Cleveland Cap Screw Company and was known for the hollow-piston valves that helped Charles Lindberg make his historic flight across the Atlantic.

From the late 1920's through the Korean War, Thompson was a leader in aircraft part manufacturing and development. They provided valves for piston engines and turbine blades for the new jet engines. So, when Ramo and Wooldridge went in search of much needed capital, it made sense to align with a company with deep pockets and a record of success with the U.S. government procurement process. Thompson fit the bill.

In 1958, the firms merged to form what is known today as Thompson, Ramo, and Wooldridge, or TRW. The list of achievements by TRW is enormous, from guided missile technology to semiconductor development and lunar module engine production. TRW had been at the forefront of American technological know-how for decades.

One little historical fact that TRW would like to ignore was their involvement in a spy case revolving around one of their contract employees, Christopher Boyce. He was a low-level communications employee in their storied Black Vault room, where encrypted communications from around the world came across through satellite and undersea cable feeds. Being the first to read many of the top-secret messages coming in from around the world gave Mr. Boyce a different perspective on the world in the mid-1970's. It appeared that not all was well in the land of Oz.

Christopher did not particularly like many of the dispatches coming out of Eastern Europe and the shenanigans being conducted by the CIA. Working in conjunction with his good friend, Andrew Daulton Lee, the two embarked on a plan to sell secrets derived from these cables to the Soviet Union. Most of the deals were conducted in Mexico City, which had a strong relationship with the Soviet Union and no reciprocity arrangement with the United States.

Boyce and Lee made pocket change for all their efforts when compared to other Soviet spies working in the United States at the time. Things were working fine until an investigation into a potential mole in the CIA uncovered communications between Christopher Boyce and a Soviet handler. William Bampen was a junior analyst in the Eastern European division of the CIA, who needed money to support his cocaine addiction and romance with a high-end escort out of Alexandria, Virginia.

Unfortunately, Christopher Boyce did not know that when he was asked to send information through a new secure channel, that the escort working Bampen was a double agent working for the CIA. It was this lead that brought the full attention of the CIA on the whereabouts of Boyce and Lee, known officially by their KGB code names—the Falcon and the Snowman.

Carle's position did require a full background check with security clearances, but rarely did he ever come across any highly classified material. TRW had won a big contract to help support the Space Shuttle program and some smaller contracts related to guidance controls for the new cruise missile, but Carle had too much integrity to even think about sharing the information. Besides, he was having too much fun. He would work early in the morning until late afternoon and then run, swim, and surf at the beach until the evening. Yep, life couldn't have been any better.

Well, until Grandpa Harper came to visit.

"Why you be wasting your life running and surfing at the beach?" Grandpa Harper asked.

"I'm not wasting my life. I work extremely hard at my job," said Carle. "TRW is one of the leading space and missile contractors in the world."

"Humph, never heard of any company worth beans that only has letters in their name."

"What about IBM or ATT?" responded Carle.

"That's different."

"Ain't no different, unless, you want it to be different, Grandpa," Carle said solemnly.

"I thought you wanted to make a difference in the world?" said Grandpa Harper.

"I do," Carle said.

"Well, then get off your ass and look around for something better. I don't see any of this space shit doing anything for the Black man," Grandpa Harper railed.

Grandpa Harper saw things so differently than most people. But he did have a point, Carle thought. In thinking of the space program, from the astronauts to the computer engineers for the lunar guidance system at TRW, it was pretty much a white thing.

Carle had gotten lazy, enjoying the easy life at TRW and the beaches of south Los Angeles county. He had fallen into the trap of being privileged—not impacted by the violence and bigotry experienced by other Black people living in Southern California and Los Angeles in particular. Carle recalled the news article about "Operation Hammer" conducted in 1987 by the Los Angeles Police Department.

It was supposed to be the definitive action about the power and might of the Los Angeles Police Department, a statement to the gangs of Los Angeles, brown and black, that their time was over. But in the end, all they could show for their efforts was just a few ounces of marijuana and some cocaine. The destruction of the homes and lives of the people impacted was just an unintended consequence. Just like the 33% increase in police brutality against people of color that followed.

It was time for him to make a difference, and he knew exactly how he would get started. Recently, his supervisor at TRW mentioned that Carle should take advantage of the educational support program being implemented for minorities. TRW would pay employees to complete an undergraduate degree or pursue advanced graduate studies. What better way for the Carle to take care of himself and help the less fortunate than by having TRW pay for him to go to law school.

Over the next few months, Carle finished up some necessary coursework at the local community college in preparation for the LSAT exam. The LSAT was an important factor in the law school application process, but Carle was always good at taking tests and he felt confident that he could score high on the exam. While he considered going back East for law school, the long history of Southwestern Law School, located in downtown Los Angeles, made it an easy choice. Southwestern had been helping people of color enter the law profession for over 50 years. And besides, it allowed Carle to stay in Los Angeles and surf those golden beaches.

CHAPTER 7

Downtown, Los Angeles, California
January, 1993

I spent a couple of months traveling around Europe during the winter months of 1993 after graduating from Cal State Northridge in December of 1992. I had pushed hard to finish that fall term and was ready for a change of scenery. I had always enjoyed looking at the older buildings of Los Angeles and was excited to see what the famous European cities had to offer.

To walk the streets of Europe was a dream come true. Besides the old churches and buildings from the 14th and 15th centuries, I was excited to look at the great works of the Renaissance painters from Italy and France. The works of Michelangelo, Titian, Raphael, and Da Vinci hung within the great museums of Rome, Paris, and London. It was an experience that would later come to play an integral role in my life.

In the excitement of my first day at the law firm, I accidentally stepped in front of a Metro bus on Wilshire Boulevard. Luckily, a guy pulled me out of the way with both of us tumbling to the sidewalk.

"Holy crap, brother. You're gonna get yourself killed around here if you don't watch what you're doing!" the guy shouted as he quickly returned to his feet with me laid out flat on the sidewalk.

"You're the new guy, right? Grant or something?" he said.

"Nigel, my name is Nigel. Nigel Grant. And, thank you," I wheezed, thinking how close I came to being another stupid pedestrian statistic. "What?"

"You okay? Did you hit your head on the pavement?" Carle said, looking at me with concern.

"No, I'm good. Just embarrassed. Thanks again." Slowly I stood up, brushing the dirt and rocks off my suit.

"Have we met? How do you know my name?" It seemed odd that he knew my name.

"No, we haven't met. My name's Carle Harper. I'm on the onboarding team for Camarena, Chavez, and Rosenberg, and I remember your face from the bio we have on you," Carle said. "I'm in charge of helping the interns get settled in."

"Well, you did one hell of a job helping this intern stay alive," I remarked, wondering how he could have remembered my face. I didn't recall submitting a photograph with my application.

"Can I buy you lunch later today?" I asked.

"Some other time. We've got to get into the office for case reports, and they usually go through lunch time," he said striding towards the office tower.

I noticed that he had a slight limp in his right leg, but still seemed to glide easily at a fast pace. I had to run to keep up with him. As I got closer, I realized how solid he looked, about 6'3" and over 230 pounds.

"Slow down, please," I said out of breath.

"Man, you don't want to be late when the boss is in the crowd. That is sure as hell one way to get your ass fired."

The way he said "the boss" made me think of Don Corleone in *The Godfather*.

We spun through the revolving doors and jetted up the escalator. We entered the conference room, already full, and apparently in session. Sitting at the head of the table was what I assume was the boss, Alphonso Camarena. Silver black hair, dark set eyes, strong nose, in what looked like an Armani suit.

The boss looked at us entering the door. "Sorry, Mr. Camarena. We were delayed by an incident at the bus stop," Carle remarked, sliding into a chair at the back of the room and pulling me down next to him.

The boss nodded his head in confirmation. "Okay, Carle. Thanks for taking care of Mr. Grant. I'm sure you mentioned my distaste for tardiness!" the boss growled, his eyes piercing right through me.

Shit. He knows my name. Carle just nodded yes, turning to me with a "you owe me more than lunch" smirk.

"Okay, let's get back to the task at hand," the boss commanded. "Ms. Vazquez was reviewing the status of the case against the Los Angeles County Sheriff's Department. We've been brought in as legal counsel by the Lakewood School District and the parents of the young men who were arrested to help prepare against criminal charges and something to do with faces... Damn it. Olivia! What is the term?"

"Eigenface assessment," Olivia said. "That is the academic term, although it is starting to be called biometrics."

I remembered hearing her say "biometrics" and thinking how lucky I was to be in that room. Only later did I realize how unlucky that would be!

Carle and I got to know each other better over the next month. Besides talking about women and baseball, he put a little perspective on what to expect from my time at the law firm.

"Basically, do what is asked of you," he said one day. "Work hard, don't complain, and you will come away with a great experience and a nice letter of recommendation from Mr. Camarena."

"Really?" I said. "I was kind of hoping for a little more than just a letter of recommendation."

"You'll get what you put into it," he said. "It ain't gonna be easy."

"I've never had it easy," I commented. "I learned that growing up being somewhat overweight. For some reason, being chubby always got me in trouble."

"Is that it?" Carle questioned.

"What do you mean, 'is that it'?" I replied.

"You're telling me you had a rough life because you were chubby?!" exclaimed Carle.

"Well, yeah. I know today it might not seem such a big deal, but it was to me," I said in my defense.

"Nah, you might have been chubby, but you were still privileged," Carle said. "So, don't tell me you had it rough because you don't know suffering unless you grew up Black."

Carle grew up in the Collier Heights part of Atlanta, a neighborhood where the elite Blacks tried to live the American Dream—a dream imagined by a local man of God. But it was still elusive to even the most learned of Black men. Martin Luther King, Jr. grew up in Atlanta and went to Morehouse College before embarking on his quest for equality and justice. However, living in such a neighborhood still did not shield Carle from racism and bigotry.

With a family legacy that stretched back to the days of the antebellum, Carle had some mighty big shoes to fill. His great-grandfather was one of the first Black men to graduate from Howard University Law School, and his grandfather was a respected attorney who fought for the rights of all men and women.

So, it might seem that Carle's dad, Solomon Carter Harper, would continue the family tradition and help people of color fight against oppression and racism through the courts. But it was not to be. With a father who challenged almost everything in a society that did not like change, Solomon's life was filled with anger and frustration. In fact, Solomon did not like law, although he knew enough about the law to get him into trouble one too many times. "Nothing like a Black man knowing more about the law, than the man himself," he was told repeatedly.

No, for Solomon his path to help the oppressed and the impoverished was through the study of medicine. For him, the rules were set by the divine creator himself.

Carle's dad would say, "The creator made us all the same. It is the world that man built that makes us different."

Reluctantly, Solomon's father let him pursue his dream of becoming a physician, helping him with the introduction to people in Nashville, Tennessee, where Meharry Medical College was located. Meharry Medical College had been training Black physicians for over 75 years and was one of the best teaching schools in the South. It started out as the medical division out of Central Tennessee College in 1876, funded through the efforts of the Methodist Episcopal Church to serve the needs of the newly freed slaves and the less fortunate of all races.

While Solomon trained to be a physician, he still was confronted by the stark reality of racism and inequality still prevalent in Tennessee while attending medical school during the turbulent 1960s. Solomon wanted to serve the health needs for all that came through his door. But eventually, he found that whites had a prejudice against seeing a Black physician. He was considered inferior and unworthy of the title. Frustrated and angry, Solomon sought counsel from his white colleagues. True to their white privilege, they would most always suggest that perhaps he should stick with taking care of his own kind.

Infuriated, this experience led Solomon to look elsewhere for a place to practice medicine. He eventually went home to Atlanta, a city that he knew and one that was moving towards a more tolerant future. A future where, hopefully, people of color could have the opportunity to govern and achieve that which was promised so long ago. The newly opened Morehouse Medical Education Program offered such opportunity for Solomon and his family.

It was no surprise then, when it came time for Carle to go to university in 1983, that Morehouse College would be his first and only choice. As the top running back in the state of Georgia, Carle had the opportunity to attend any number of football programs in the United States. But for Carle, it didn't really matter. All he ever wanted to do was play football at Morehouse College and get drafted by his beloved Atlanta Falcons.

But that dream went away in a flash during his senior year against Alabama A & M, one play that changed his life path forever. Naturally, having a father teach at the local medical school meant that Carle had access to the best surgeon in town when it came time to fix his knee.

"Yep, the knee is pretty much gone," commented Dr. Johnson, head of the surgical unit at Atlanta General Hospital, looking at the x-ray.

"We know that much, Rufus," said Solomon, "but will he be able to walk normally?"

Doc Johnson looked over at Carle and then at Solomon. "Sol, I've known you going on 10 years now," Doc Johnson frowned, shaking his head. "I will do everything in my power to make that knee good, but I can't guarantee that he won't have a little limp. There's just too much damage."

"Amen," Solomon crowed, "we can live with a little limp."

Carle sat patiently, taking it all in. "If I redshirt this season, can I play next year?" Carle yelled.

Solomon and Doc Johnson jumped, startled by the loudness of Carle's question.

"Son, what Doc Johnson is saying," Solomon comforted his son, "is that your days of playing football are over."

"No, it can't be!" Carle shouted, his voice trailing off to a whisper, "I need to play, so I can get drafted."

Both men stared at the young man, wise in their years, knowing when best to be quiet.

Eventually, Solomon rose from his chair and placed an arm around his son, "It's okay, Carle. The good Lord will lead you down another path."

And, with that, Carle's dream was over.

It took about two months for Carle to be able to place any weight on his right knee, and by then it was Christmas break with Carle closing out 1986 sitting in the Morehouse University library working on a paper about the inequality of trade between nations.

With a focus on getting drafted by the Falcons, Carle never really thought much about what he would do as an alternative. However, it seemed that classes in the business department came easy, and he liked the structure of contract law. In fact, the more he learned about the illegal actions of corporations and people, the more he liked considering a career in the legal profession.

"Why don't you go out to California, and visit your cousin, Wayne?" his mom, Letha, suggested one day, sensing an unease in her son.

"I read an article in *Reader's Digest* talking about the growing opportunities in Los Angeles," she said confidently, "and Wayne works at some aerospace company by the airport. You could probably stay with him and figure out what you want to do."

"Now, Letha, don't you go tempting our son with all those fine-looking California Girls roller skating on the beach," whistled Solomon, ducking from the oven-mitt tossed his way, but also giving a little wink to Carle.

By the summer of 1987, Carle had moved out to California, but he was not living with Wayne. Come to find out that Wayne did not work in the aerospace industry, but the movie industry. And, not the kind of movies his mom and dad watched on TV.

Nevertheless, with money he had saved up during college, Carle was able to get himself an apartment in Manhattan Beach, a sleepy beach suburb of Los Angeles, favored by the upper middle-class workers from the aerospace industry in the nearby towns of Hawthorne, Redondo Beach, and El Segundo.

He was two blocks from the beach, where he could work out the kinks in his right knee by running in the sand. It gave him plenty of time to think about his future.

CHAPTER 8

Camarena, Chavez, and Rosenberg Office
Los Angeles, California
February, 1993

"Olivia, you were saying," Alphonso said, jolting Olivia out of her Palm Springs daydream.

She had been thinking about her life and how her parents made the sacrifice so long ago to give her a better life. They had settled in the desert town of Indio in the late 1960's when "Coachella" meant desert, not music festival.

Living close to Palm Springs allowed her father, Manuel Vasquez, to find work at one of the remaining tennis resorts in town. The history of tennis in the area went back to the golden age of the 1920's, when the Hollywood celebrities would drive out for the clean air and a nice game of tennis. Those times ended by the time Olivia and her parents arrived, but there was still some interest in tennis.

While not old enough to work, Olivia did get the opportunity to earn pocket money delivering her special iced mint tea with sliced oranges to the many celebrities and movie stars who frequented the tennis resort. As she blossomed into a young woman, it seemed natural that Olivia would take up tennis. While her forehand could have gotten her into any of the top ranked university tennis programs developing at the time, it was her intellect and grades that got her noticed by the Pepperdine University recruiter.

Coming back to the present, Olivia wished she was back in college. Pepperdine was a great school and the classes challenging, but nothing like the stress of working at Camarena, Chavez, and Rosenburg. This case was giving her a lot of challenges and heartburn.

"Olivia," said her boss, Alphonso. "Explain to me how in hell they're going to match the composite drawings again?"

"Sit down, sir. This is going to take a while," Olivia says motioning him to sit in the chair.

She knew that Mr. Camarena had seen many cases related to civil liberty violations, but she doubted very much that he had experienced anything like this before in his life.

Alphonso, as he was known around East Los Angeles, was a thin, muscular man. Being from a devout Catholic family, he was fortunate that the angels and his family looked after him. Growing up in East LA and the surrounding area was not conducive to a long life for people of color. It was a battle between the forces of good and evil. Naturally, one thought of law enforcement as good and gangs as evil, but this wasn't necessarily accurate. Often, their roles were reversed.

Sadly, for Alphonso, his older brother, Enrique, died at the hands of the police, while his younger brother, Rubio, died trying to prevent gangs from recruiting a friend in their neighborhood. Alphonso turned 18 around the time that Ruby was killed, and it forced him to realize that his future looked bleak if he stayed in East LA. Luckily, a Marine Corps recruiter

by the name of Gonzalez came to his high school the week after Ruby's funeral. The recruiter was dressed in full Marine
Corps uniform, looking sharp and squared-away, which
helped Alphonso realize there was another path.

Climbing into the bus headed for Camp Pendleton in 1967,
Alphonso looked at his mother and father, wondering if he
would ever see them again. He prayed for their safety and
promised to God that he would return and help the less fortunate fight the forces of good and evil.

Fifty-six months later, Sergeant Alphonso Camarena got
discharged out of the United States Marine Corps in June of
1972. He had spent almost five years in the Marine Corps with
two 13-month deployments to Vietnam.

It was time to use the G.I. Bill to go to school and to become
an attorney. In Alphonso's mind, that was the only way he
could make good and evil pay for their sins of the past!

"So, you're telling me that the Los Angeles Sheriff's Department was brought in by the Lakewood Police Department to
match composite drawings with pictures of high school students?" Alphonso asked, "Hoping to identify a few boys
charged with rape and assault? Do I read this correctly?"

"Yes, sir," Olivia responded calmly, knowing that this kind of
stuff set the boss off on a rant about privacy protection and constitutional rights. "Evidently, the girls who have come forward can't
clearly identify the perpetrators, so the hope was that an illustrator
could generate a reasonable likeness for identification and then
match it with photographs from the high school yearbook!"

"Is that true?" the boss whispered under his breath, not believing what he just heard.

Olivia exclaimed, "It is the truth, *jefe*."

"And, why did they ask the Los Angeles Sheriff's Department?" questioned the boss.

"Well, that is the interesting part," Olivia grinned, "the Sheriff's Department had been requested by the Department of Justice to test a new digitizing computer process to match mugshots with standard-composite drawings taken from Los Angeles County criminal files."

The boss looked at her as if she were speaking some foreign dialect, "Say that again!"

"First you have to understand the history of Lakewood and the problems at the high school," Olivia commented, explaining to her boss.

"The city of Lakewood was born out of the aerospace industry that had built up around Los Angeles during World War II. The factories of Douglas Aircraft, North American Aviation, and Northrop Aircraft needed workers to keep the economic machine running, and homes were a major factor in that machine for the tens of thousands of returning GI's coming through the ports of Los Angeles and Long Beach.

"The Servicemen's Readjustment Act of 1944 provided funding for rehabilitation hospitals, granted stipends for college tuition and expenses, and funded low interest mortgages. The G.I. Bill, the popular name of the Act, offered the opportunity of a lifetime for the returning servicemen or so it seemed.

"To satisfy the demand for housing, a group of businessmen combined forces to turn former bean and sugar beet farmland in South Los Angeles into over 17,500 single-family homes. The housing development would be a master-planned community that would include schools and parks, and the new concept of a regional shopping center, anchored by a large department store ready to capture the needs of the newly employed and growing families.

"And, boy, did they come, beginning with the opening of the Cimarron subdivision in late 1950. Lakewood exploded onto the scene of suburbia. Growth continued unabated for the next thirty years as the end of World War II melded with the confluence of the Korean War and the Vietnam campaign.

"War meant business to the companies around Lakewood: the old stalwarts like Douglas and Northrup and the newer breeds of Hughes Corporation, TRW, and Rockwell. Not only was aerospace booming, but the march to the moon and beyond brought thousands of new jobs to Rockwell and Hughes Aircraft during the 1960's and early 1970's, creating an endless need for engineers, secretaries, laborers, and mill workers.

"As the urban sprawl began to push out further towards the surrounding towns of Carson, Compton, and Bellflower, the lack of jobs for people of color and racial inequality were magnified by the G.I. Bill itself. The VA loans promised to the returning veterans were not managed by the VA but by white-run financial institutions who used covert racist covenants and common red-lining practices to exclude Blacks from certain neighborhoods. Lakewood was one of these neighborhoods.

"By the late 1980's, the ugly historic practices used to keep Blacks out of Lakewood and other white communities had ended. The world and Lakewood were changing, the morals and culture of the past replaced by something unknown and foreign. Rules were to be broken, boundaries pushed to the max, and lives shaken to their core.

"Interestingly, the boundaries being pushed were not along the lines of color but of gender. And, it became never more apparent than during the summer of 1992 when the Posse started their game. At first, it was just rumors: young high school boys doing what young boys have always done. But it became a little more troubling when it was released that they had developed a "point system" for their sexual conquests—a point-system that placed them in a hierarchy of who was a player and who was not!

"Soon the stories being told included intimidation, coercion, and rape with a few entering the world of burglary and robbery. But, even then, the residents of Lakewood and the parents of these young males, now in college and preparing to enter the world, did not want to acknowledge what their city and offspring had become.

"Eventually, enough was enough. When information came out that one of the sexual assault victims was a 10-year-old girl, it was only then that the city, the parents, and the school, realized they had a problem, but by then it was too late. The 'golden land,' as Lakewood had once been called, was forever gone!"

The story of Lakewood could be played out in countless towns and neighborhoods associated with the aviation industry after WWII. Over time, the idyllic notion of the American Dream was replaced by the ugliness of segregation and inequality. It just happened that the Posse brought the notion of white privilege into the living room of every person in the world.

"Basically, the residents of the affluent communities in California were oblivious to the events taking place in the cities around them," said Olivia.

"What do you mean by 'events around them'?" asked Alphonso.

"Incidences of profiling, police brutality, unfair search and seizure, and surveillance that were occurring on a daily basis," Olivia said, "and all related to a shared trait."

"And that was?" Alphonso requested.

"They were all poor and predominantly Black," Olivia shared.

PART FOUR

CHAPTER 9

Clare looked around the room one more time before closing the door. She was going to miss this apartment – it had a great view of the pool and had easy access to the 405 freeway. She wasn't much for cooking, so it was nice to have some good restaurants within walking distance for takeout down on Ventura Boulevard.

It was better than that dive she lived in when she was working in Maryland during her last assignment. This assignment in Los Angeles had been one of the shortest, but she really enjoyed the three years living in the San Fernando Valley. The proximity to Los Angeles and the beaches were some of the many benefits, not to mention being near her brother, Charles.

It wasn't like she got to see him a lot, but every now and then, they would get together for breakfast down the street at Jerry's Delicatessen. It was a special day when he would bring his kids, which wasn't all that often. For some reason, Clare didn't get along with his wife, Brenda, who thought Clare's work life was a bit transitory for her liking.

In fact, Clare would agree that her work life sucked, but it paid the bills. And, with the medical and housing expenses for her mom, there were a lot of bills to pay. She only wished she could see her mom more often, but given all the travel restrictions it wasn't that easy to get over to France. And besides, she didn't get enough time off for leisure travel to get over there and back to make it worthwhile.

Checking to make sure the door was locked, Clare shouldered her backpack and grabbed the handle of her suitcase. The beauty of renting a furnished apartment meant that when it was time to go, there was no need for packing boxes and moving vans.

Walking down the stairs, Clare could see the apartment complex manager looking out his window and cringed at having to speak with him. He was perhaps the most disgusting person she had ever met. The way he looked at her when she left in the morning and then at night when she came home was dis-concerting.

"You clean the carpets and kitchen?" he asked.

"Yes, Karl. I did everything you requested. I sure hope I can get some of my deposit back."

"Hey, I told you we could work something out," Karl said suggestively pulling at his crotch. "I got some beer chillin' in the fridge."

"Ah, you know I would consider your offer, but I gotta get down to San Diego before noon," Clare said. "Maybe next time I come up we can work something out."

"Sure, I can hold off on processing that final deposit for you," Karl smiled. "Just let me know when you are back in town, Gloria. We can have a little fun!"

Clare gave him a little wave and headed off to her car thinking about his offer. *Yes, we might have a little fun, but not the kind of fun you're thinking, pervert.*

Stepping into the front seat of her rental car, Clare did one more look around. The drive to San Diego would take about three hours, and she didn't want to stop. Her contact at the agency told her that she had to report for her new assignment by late afternoon. The on-boarding process would take most of the afternoon, and she still needed to scope out the target.

The agency was putting her up at some hotel in Del Mar, which was supposed to be close to the company headquarters. Hopefully, it wouldn't take her long to figure out her job duties, so she could get an apartment or small house nearby. The notion of a nice cozy beach house was comforting after several years of living out of a suitcase.

Looking in the rear-view mirror one more time, Clare stepped on the gas and headed out of the apartment complex. It was a straight shot down Hayvenhurst Boulevard to the Ventura Freeway and another life—one of many that she has had over the past 20 years.

CHAPTER 10

Face Value Headquarters
San Diego, California
December 22, 2020

"Okay, Nigel. Welcome to Face Value," Greta said, the traditional handshake replaced by a fist bump. "If you have any questions, just check in with my new assistant, Clare."

l stood up and accepted the bump. Wondering what to do next.

"I think you were going to meet Bernadette down in the cafeteria. Right?" Greta reminded me.

"Oh, yeah. My mind is a little fuzzy with everything going on. Thanks," I said. l gave her my most radiant smile and slowly left through the office door.

"Hey, you." l heard and turned to see Bernadette coming towards him, "You ready for that lunch?"

"You bet! I'm starved," l responded. "Thanks for taking me to the cafeteria."

The little bistro area down in the lobby still had some reminders of the coronavirus pandemic fear. The tables were still spread far apart, and there were signs outlining appropriate social distancing spread among them.

The kitchen area itself still had the plexiglass panels separating the workers from the people moving along the food line with their trays. The old 'X marks the spot' were still plastered on the floor, although with the new Federal rules, they were obsolete.

The cafeteria itself was pretty much what you would find in a corporate office building anywhere in the United States, except for the fresh fruit, Kombucha offerings, and an open bar with wine and draft beer on tap. Over lunch l got to know Bernadette a little better, not realizing all the things we had in common.

l shared that my father had been in the Air Force, so we moved around quite a bit. Bernadette mentioned that she had grown up in San Diego. Her father had been in the Navy, stationed at Coronado Island. She understood the challenges of moving around every few years.

She went to the local community college in San Diego, unsure of what to do and unwilling to move again when her dad got orders to move up to Bremerton, Washington. She stayed behind, going to school, and working for a small biotech company in the emerging Sorrento Valley area near the swanky town of La Jolla.

It was from that job that got her into the University of San Diego, a private Catholic school that had good academics and an even better reputation for getting alumni jobs. Before we knew it, an hour flew by, and it was time for Bernadette to meet another candidate.

"When is your meeting with Doc?" asked Bernadette, using the more informal term for Professor Gallegos.

"I think Greta said in a couple of weeks," l reflected. "I need to go back to Portland and finish up a couple of things before I start."

"Well, you might want to make sure," Bernadette said.

"Yes, you are correct." l said glumly, "I will go back to Greta's office and verify the time."

Bernadette stood up and picked up their trays. "Well, come on then. Let's walk up to HR together," she said with such a pretty smile.

We took the elevator up to the second floor, unconsciously standing on the big blue Xs painted on the elevator floor. While the world was slowly coming out of the pandemic paranoia, it was evident that much of what we had been experiencing over the past year had become normal behavior.

"Okay, here you go," Bernadette said as we approached Human Resources. "I have a meeting in a few minutes down the hall. Welcome to the team."

"Thanks. For everything!" l replied.

Bernadette smiled and turned away.

"Would it be possible to meet for lunch when I come back?" l blurted out.

"Perhaps," Bernadette chimed, looking back with a mischievous grin. "Now, go on and verify that time."

l grabbed the doorknob. Taking a big breath, I turned the knob and pushed the door open, expecting to see Greta, the Blonde Goddess.

"Uh, hello," l stuttered, realizing that before me stood not Greta, but the woman from yesterday with incredible emerald green eyes floating above a stylish face covering.

"Hellooo, can I help you?" she said.

l stared, frozen. "Yes, my name is Nigel Grant," I said sheepishly. "I was checking on my appointment time with Professor Gallegos."

"Oh, yes. The new candidate from yesterday. That sounded like some argument you were having with Bernadette," she said pulling down her face covering. "What was that all about?"

"Oh, it was nothing, really," I said. "Just some gibberish about a project I worked on a very long time ago."

"What kind of project?" she asked.

"Something about stealth technology and face recognition. All hush-hush," I whispered.

"Ah, okay" she said with a wink. "Forgotten!"

I stood there trying to remember her name and feeling a bit awkward.

"My name is Clare," she said. "Welcome. Today is my first full day, but I think I can figure out the calendar."

She poked around on her keyboard, looking up at me every now and then. "You don't seem distracted."

"Beg, your pardon?" I questioned.

"Greta said that you come across distracted at times, but that in fact you were coded as an Authenticator III," Clare said. "She seemed quite surprised."

I stood, pacing back and forth, wondering what to say.

"Oh, never mind," said Clare, her eyes sparkling with the ceiling lights. "It says here that your appointment is January 11th at 10 AM. Professor Gallegos wants to meet you in his office on the 5th floor."

"Thanks again...," long pause.

"My name is Clare Marie. But you can call me Clare."

"Yes, thanks again, Clare," I said, walking out the door.

CHAPTER 11

Portland, Oregon
December 31, 2020

I spent the next couple of days in San Diego enjoying the beach and the Gaslamp Quarter again before heading back to Portland to attend a friend's New Year's Eve party. I still couldn't believe that I came down to San Diego for a holiday and came away with a new job. It had been a long time since I had been actively employed, and I was anxious to get started.

The interview at Face Value had been strange, but then again, for that kind of money, it was worth it. And, there was one thing that I needed to do right away. Unfortunately, that meant contacting my ex-wife, Jennifer. We didn't have the best relationship after our divorce, but I owed her some money that up until six days ago, I didn't have nor did I have any way to pay her back.

But that had all changed with that little poster at the Portland Airport. Thank God!

"Hi, Jen. It's Nigel," I said to my ex, waiting for my flight back to Portland.

"I know who it is! You show up on my phone under Asshole," Jennifer answered, always one with a snarky comment. "What do you want Nigel?"

"Well, I just got a full-time job, so I will be able to pay you the money I owe you sooner than planned," l said, feeling the satisfaction of telling her.

Silence on the other end. "Jennifer, are you there?" I asked.

"Uh, yes," Jennifer stammered.

"Can we meet later in the week. I'll tell you all about it?" I said.

"Why sure, how about you come over on Saturday, and I will fix us lunch here at the house," Jennifer said.

"Sounds perfect. See you around noon then," l responded.

Besides meeting with Jennifer, I needed to inform the department chair at Portland State that I wouldn't be able to teach this term or ever again. She wasn't going to like hearing the news, but for the money I was getting paid at Face Value, it was worth her grief.

The drive into downtown Portland from the airport on Interstate 84 can be brutal, which is why I normally take the Max Train. I noticed that the ridership seemed smaller than normal, perhaps due to the social distancing thing with the coronavirus scare. It was amazing to me that most people were still cautious around crowds. I think if you haven't been infected by now, something is wrong with you.

Thankfully, it wasn't raining, so I enjoyed looking from the light rail car window at all the cars approaching the Interstate 84 and I-5 split. It was not a very well-thought-out interchange, but then again, it was never expected that Portland would grow to become such a large metropolitan region.

Portland was meant to be a small town. And, like the Peter Gabriel song,

> *The place where I come from is a small town*
> > *They think so small*
> > > *They use small words.*

Small town thinkers tended to be small town planners. And, as far as I could tell, there really wasn't a hint of any planning when it came to roads or housing in the Portland metro area.

When Jen and I finally divorced in 2012, I was barely able to scrape up money for a down payment on a small, one-bedroom condo in the Pearl District. The down payment came from my parents who weren't financially well off, but they were able to help a little bit. l didn't really want to take the money, but I was kind of desperate.

Without their contribution, I wouldn't have been able to swing the deal. Now, that deal seems like good fortune. My father just said, "I'd rather watch you enjoy it while I'm living, than from my grave."

The Pearl had turned into quite the destination for the TripAdvisor crowd. My one-bedroom condo was worth considerably more than what I had paid almost eight years ago. I just hoped that my good fortune in Portland didn't end like my experience in Boston. I mean at the time in 2005, the Boston condo seemed like a good idea, just like the Portland condo seemed like a good idea in 2012. And, now it appeared that the coronavirus was going to crush the economy again. Just my luck!

Sitting in the Max train and crossing the Willamette River near the Rose Quarter, I remembered the first time I met

Jennifer. I had gone out with some friends to celebrate our third year of employment with the investment firm. The place to be and be seen in 2004 at the time was the Boston Harbor Hotel, across the street from the famous Quincy Market and Faneuil Hall.

Jennifer was waiting to order a drink at the Rowes Wharf Bar in the hotel and seemed a bit agitated.

"What d'ya think I'm do-ing here?" she yelled at the bartender. "I've been waitin' to get a fucking drink for about 20 minutes. You go take a smoke or something?"

l didn't hear what the bartender said, but I definitely heard Jen's response.

"You little mother fucker. I have a mind to jump over that bar and kick your fucking ass!"

She started climbing over the bar until l intervened. "Whoa! Let's not get that pretty dress all dirty," I said trying to smooth things over. "I'm sure we can get…Gary here to get you a drink on the house."

"What do you say about that Gary?" l said, trying to cool things down, sliding a twenty over the bar top.

"Sure, I can help the little lady with her drink." Gary shrugged, then shouted, "Fucking bitch."

And, with that, Jen launched over the bar punching Gary right in the nose. I still don't know why I did it, but it took a lot of talking to get Gary to not press charges and all the cash I had in my wallet.

They say love is blind, and evidently, I was blind as a bat.

I am not a big fan of the weather in Portland during January. The weather tends to be a bit cold and unpredictable. You can have blue skies or grey skies with rain and about the same temperature–30 degrees.

To make matters worse, the Pearl District had taken a big hit from the coronavirus outbreak. A good number of the small bars and nationally-acclaimed restaurants near my condo had closed. A few remained, but in general most Portlanders still did not feel comfortable going into town for an evening of pub-crawling and dining. The prospects of me making bank on my condo was looking bleaker every single day.

If the fancy apartments in the Pearl District were struggling, one could only imagine how difficult it must be out in East Portland. The west side had the money from Nike and Intel to keep the dream alive. Sadly, the eastside consisted mostly of pot shops and tattoo parlors, plus a smattering of old mom and pop businesses that should have closed shop decades ago. This precarious image of Portland was not something you heard about on national news, and sadly at times, not from the local media either.

When the world was in freefall in 2009, Portland was where Jen wanted to be. Her job at Emerson had gotten eliminated due to low student enrollment, and my position at the investment firm was tenuous at best. The amount of free cash available for investment ideas dried up almost immediately in 2008.

The firm hadn't done a deal in over a year, and there was talk of closing shop. Eventually, the partners decided to pull up stakes and move on to other opportunities. Along with the other employees, I got a decent severance package. It wasn't the kind of money to allow me to not to ever work again, but at least I didn't have to worry about how to cover our Boston house payment for a while.

Well, that was when we thought it would sell fast. But, six months later, the cash pile started to dwindle, and the discussion about walking away from our condo became a weekly argument between Jen and me. Luckily, just when I had given up any hope of selling, we finally got a price that allowed us to break even. Little did I know that was only the start of my downward spiral. That spiral lasted almost 11 years and took just about every shred of self-confidence and zest for life that I had.

I had spent most of yesterday informing various business contacts and friends that I would be moving down to San Diego. The Portland State department chair had given me a bunch of crap for bailing on her, but she understood when I told her about the money I was going to make. With the university having reduced enrollment for the winter quarter, I think she was glad that I was leaving.

By Saturday afternoon, I was starting to feel good about the decision to move to San Diego. The time to leave Portland had come, and it felt really good as the Uber driver crossed over the Willamette heading towards my old house. A house that had more bad memories than good.

Crossing the Sellwood bridge, the car turned right on SE 9th Street from Tacoma Avenue and headed towards the single-story bungalow at the cross-section of SE Harney Street. Seeing the house from the street, I noticed a few changes to the front lawn, nothing major except for the removal of the raised flower bed, which was sad because I had spent considerable time building that planter box.

Sellwood was charming and historic, but not car friendly. It was considered a good day in when you found a parking spot close to home. The car pulled up to the curb, and I thanked the driver while closing the car door. I walked slowly up to the front door thinking that perhaps this wasn't such a good idea.

"Hello, stranger. About time, you got here," Jen said, eliminating any chance of me going back to the car. She had a wine glass in one hand and her smart phone in the other.

"Hello," l replied cordially. "Glad you got the party started."

Jen's drinking was always an issue and one of the main reasons why we divorced.

"Screw you, Nigel. Are you going to lecture me again?" she shouted, the anger and bitterness still present.

"Jen, I don't want to fight," l said.

Jen stepped away from the archway and walked back towards the front room. l always liked the layout of this house. It had a small foyer for greeting guests and hanging jackets. Off to the left was the hall down to the two bedrooms.

On the right was a nice formal living room area adjacent to the kitchen and dining area. Through the kitchen you could see the lush backyard through the French doors. It was those French doors that sold me when Jennifer called me that summer of 2009. She had flown out early to get an idea of the real estate market. I had stayed behind in Boston to finish up at the investment firm and pack up the U-Haul. Money was so tight that we decided the best way to move was do-it-yourself.

"I want this house, Nigel," Jen said over the phone. "It has the most magical backyard, and I think you'll really like the layout of the kitchen and French doors that look onto the back."

"Does the realtor think our offer will be accepted?" l asked.

"Yes, she thinks that the offer is solid and that the owners are in desperate need to sell." The joy of another's misfortune was alive in Jens's voice.

"Okay, let's go for it," I responded, worried more about packing and getting on the road than the house.

I was somewhere around Illinois when I got her call, "They accepted our offer and agreed to the 30-day escrow," Jen squealed over the phone.

"That's great," l sighed. And, now standing in the kitchen eleven years later, I could see why my life was in shambles. The kitchen counter was full of wine bottles and beer cans. There were pizza containers and take-away boxes from the Thai restaurant around the corner.

I realized now that had I listened, really listened back in Boston when I first met Jennifer, I would have heard the conductor say…

"All aboard the crazy train!"

PART FIVE

CHAPTER 12

Los Angeles, California
Mid-February, 1993

The early 1990s brought an unprecedented influx of people and money to Southern California. White, brown, and black, they all came to take advantage of the growing economy. Some were citizens and some were not. In the end it did not matter, they all eventually became impacted by the burgeoning drug trade.

When drugs arrive, gangs soon follow. Where there are gangs, there are territories that need to be protected which eventually leads to death. The police and sheriff departments throughout California and, in Los Angeles in particular, were becoming swamped with crimes of all kinds. Some leading to arrests and some not. It just depended upon who had the time to piece it all together.

It wasn't like any of this was new to those in law enforcement. Most of the Black and Hispanic gangs had been around in California since the 1920's, and it was known that white gangs had been around even longer. What was new to the equation was the increasing number of Asian gangs representing countries like Vietnam, Laos, and Cambodia. And, the deadly MS-13 gang was starting to make its name known throughout Southern California for the most violent of crimes.

Given the wide variety of ethnicities within the gang community, it was unpleasant and awkward to see the specific focus on the Black gangs. For many in law enforcement it was felt that there had to be an all-encompassing approach to the problem, but for the Los Angeles Police Department it became clear–the focus was just on Black crime.

The Los Angeles Police Department began to focus on Black crime with the launch of Operation Hammer in the summer of 1988. It soon became an example of the police brutality and racism forced upon the Black community by law enforcement agencies around the United States.

The simmering anger and frustration in the Black community came out in rage and terror on the night of April 29th in 1993. The acquittal of the four police officers in the beating of Rodney King was enough to set off the bomb, and a bomb it was, lasting for days with countless acts of violence against people of all colors. It can be said that it ended when Rodney King pleaded for us to all get along, but in reality, the anger and violence faded with fatigue and force.

This force was driven by the arrival of 6,000 National Guard and some 4,000 federal officers and Marines, allowing the LAPD and other organizations the chance to come in and take stock of the situation. Not since the Watts Riot of 1965 had Los Angeles experienced such damage and carnage. With over 3000 buildings burned or destroyed and an equal number of businesses closed, the financial and emotional cost was mind-boggling. Not to mention the 63 deaths and over 12,000 arrests.

The magnitude of arrests was beyond comprehension and belief. In addition, the sheer number was over-whelming for a criminal justice system that was antiquated and broken. Many arrests were of individuals with no known record or reliable personal identification. Without the ability to verify prior criminal activity and the need to process such a large number, many of the perpetrators were released.

Part of the problem was the archaic system of photographing and storing images for documentation, plus the ability to match or verify an image from a source document. In addition, the system offered truly little in the way of 'searchable' parameters. Luckily, the Los Angeles County Sheriff's Department had been selected by the Department of Justice in the summer of 1992 to test a new system for taking traditional photographs and scanning them for storage as a digitized file. It was hoped that this new storage format would speed up the ability to provide a level of identification not possible through fingerprints. Law enforcement around the world was learning that the value of an image, a face, if possible, was invaluable.

Using current photocopying technology, Draper Labs with the help of Carnegie Mellon University had developed an advanced software system purported to improve the pixel resolution of a scan during the digitizing process. It was a joint program funded by DARPA and the Department of Justice in support of the pending Simpson-Mazzoli Act, commonly known as the Immigration Reform and Control Act.

The Simpson-Mazzoli Act was essentially written to protect American workers from losing jobs to the large number of undocumented immigrants coming across the southern border of the United States. It was hoped that the process being developed through Draper Labs and tested with the Los Angeles Sheriff's Department would help expedite the documentation process of these immigrants.

The Immigration and Naturalization Service (INS) needed to establish a database containing images of the undocumented individuals for comparison later. It was well known that many of these hard-working immigrants would make it back into the U.S. looking for work. So, the INS needed a means to demonstrate that they were in the U.S. illegally, and the Department of Justice was hoping that the Draper Labs technology would help.

In late January 1993, it was suggested by an unknown source that the Lakewood Police Department should contact the Los Angeles Sheriff's Department about the use of the Draper Lab technology for the Posse case at Lakewood High School. The plan was to compare the composite drawings obtained by the victims with the photographs of the alleged suspects from the high school yearbook. It took a few months to create an interagency memorandum of understanding, but by February, the project was given the green light.

It was the curiosity of the new library sciences coordinator at the Lakewood High School district office that brought the project to the attention of the school district and eventually the parents. Naturally, once the parents and the school itself learned of the project, they reached out to legal counsel for guidance on how to stop the release of the yearbook photographs. It was a fortuitous request given that in a mere three weeks many of these young men would be arrested and charged with sexual assault and rape.

Sadly, the Lakewood case was starting to make national headlines because many of the alleged perpetrators started appearing on television shows geared more to shock and disgust than educate and inform–an immensely popular format in the mid-1990s.

"I wish the school district or at least the parents would stop those kids from going on national television," I said.

"Who cares? They are just trying to take advantage of their newfound popularity," Carle remarked.

"Yeah, but they run the risk of sharing too much information that can be used against them," I said. "And they are making it harder for us to maintain ownership of their likeness."

"What do you mean by likeness?" Olivia asked.

"Likeness as in 'image of themselves,'" I said. "I think there is merit in using ownership of self in their defense against the Los Angeles Sheriff's Department. It reminds me of how English royalty used portraits to establish their place in history."

"You mean to tell me that portraits from the 16th and 17th centuries were used to establish ownership of self?" Carle exclaimed while sitting in our office at the Los Angeles law firm.

"Yes," I responded. "The Egyptians had developed the technique of capturing the likeness of men and women through rudimentary sculpture in early 500 BC, which was improved by Grecians using different materials and tools."

"Wow, that is an interesting angle," chimed Carle rolling his eyes in disbelief.

"Well, the Chinese are credited with using fingerprints, handprints, and footprints for identification starting around 200 BC," I said. "So, this whole biometric concept we talk about now isn't really all that new."

Olivia glared at me, "Continue."

"Well, as part of learning about the "self," the ruling class of the Greek and Roman empires realized that in order to establish "domain" or dominance, there needed to be some material artefact, some resemblance of self, to show ownership and control," I said.

"It is why early Greek and Roman ruins are found to contain numerous busts of the citizens. To show their dominance, the landowners would commission a local artisan for a bust reflecting their likeness. As the artisans became more skilled in the process, each successive bust began to truly reflect the individual image of the owner."

I continued, "One might say that the bust reflected the first face identification system, which was used not only for ownership, but eventually identification as well. That is why in certain regions we can find busts reflecting different decades for these wealthy owners."

"Fast forward about a thousand years, and the ruling class of England and France do the same thing with stylized portraiture and eventually more informal landscapes depicting the scale and scope of the land and houses. All with the express interest of establishing their ownership!"

Carle and Olivia looked at the photocopies of the pictures I had gotten from the library. There was a bust of Socrates, a picture of Richard the Lionheart, Louis XV, and even one of George Washington.

"Why does ownership have any material relevance to our case?" Carle asked.

I looked at Olivia. "Yes, what about ownership?" she said.

"Well, when I was digging into the background about the computer software system used by the Los Angeles Sheriff's Department, it dawned on me that we were ignoring one simple fact," I said.

"And, what might that be?" Olivia asked.

"The person," I beamed with pride. "It seems intuitive that we would own our likeness, but what does the law say about ownership of self, and what is the value of a face?"

Olivia stopped in mid-stride. "Interesting, let me think about that," she said. "How about you focus on the software angle for the time being."

"Okay," I said, feeling frustrated that my idea had not gotten much accolades. The face was the key; I just needed more time to figure it out.

The following week as I walked into our office, Carle said, "Are you British or something?" He looked up from the Los Angeles Times sport section, "What's up with the name 'Nigel'?"

A good question, l thought. But not something I wanted to ponder first thing in the morning.

"You know, I'm not sure," l shrugged. "My mom says that my dad got the name from an author who wrote about the Soviet Union in 1964, and well, my dad can't remember, because of memory problems."

"Oh, I'm sorry to hear that," Carle said.

Olivia walked into the room, "Sorry to hear what?" she asked.

"Nothing," Carle and l blurted out at the same time.

Olivia stopped in her tracks, looking suspiciously at both of us. Her black hair cascading down to just above her shoulders. Those brown eyes looking at us warmly.

"You guys! Always hiding something," she frowned. She stepped around the desk and sat down.

"Okay, let's get to work. We have a lot to do before the pre-motion hearing this afternoon."

This was my first chance to work on a legal case, and I was very appreciative to land in the new privacy group headed up by Olivia. l wasn't certain about whether I wanted to pursue a legal career, but the pay was good, and I was intrigued by this case. The notion of using composite drawings to match mugshots from a computer database was unimaginable and intriguing.

l had experience with the use of IBM mainframes at Cal State Northridge during my class in statistics, and even one of my friends owned an Apple MacIntosh. But, to think that you could use composite drawings, drawn by hand, and then match them with digital images was fascinating.

"Nigel, are you listening?" Olivia queried.

Carle elbowed me in the side, "Wake up, buddy."

"Oh, sorry, I was just thinking about how the use of computers will change everything we do," l said. "It's going to make things so much easier."

Olivia and Carle looked at me, having experienced my tendency to wander off into space.

"Yeah, and it just might make our life a little less private," said Carle, shaking his head.

"Yes, that's true, Carle," Oliva stated. "But, I don't think the technology for storing large amounts of information is cost-effective at this time."

"Again, what does this have to do with our case?" asked Carle.

"In simple terms, the ability to store and sort data at lower costs will make it easier for anyone to analyze trends and patterns, not just the government," l shared.

"So what?" Carle said. "What does that have to do with composite drawings and our defense?"

"Be patient, I'm getting there," l responded. "If this goes to trial, we'll need to show that what the Lakewood Police Department and the Los Angeles Sheriff's Department are doing is egregious and against current privacy laws."

"Okay, I get it," said Olivia. "It's a complex issue, and we'll need to make sure the jurors understand the complexity and parameters involved. Nigel, what else are you thinking?"

l looked at Olivia and Carle. It is the first time that I have been considered equal in this arrangement, and it felt good.

"Well, what we need to outline is how private and public entities have been taking advantage of the laws related to personal freedom and privacy for decades," I said.

I stood up to stretch. Looking at Olivia and Carle, I outlined my thoughts,

"First, we introduce how the Materials Science Division (MSD) was created by the Defense Advanced Research Projects Agency in 1960 to understand properties related to topological surface analysis through advanced synthetic materials design.

"Second, we fast forward to the mid-1980's and the stealth jet fighter program funded by DARPA. We detail the progress that Lockheed had implementing the new composite materials and angular planes into the F-117 Nighthawk aircraft design to reduce its radar signature.

"Third, we highlight the development of information processing techniques by DARPA and Carnegie Mellon and the danger that it poses to individual freedom and privacy."

By now I was pacing back and forth in our small office suite. Hands waving, pacing, preaching to the jury.

"Okay, Nigel. Let's finish this up, so we can move on," Olivia sighed, bringing me back to Earth.

I continued, "and, the fourth connection is the development of machine learning and how it is used to understand how various shapes and surface color can be detected by radar and traditional photography."

Olivia and Carle looked at me. I said firmly,

"and, that's how we show how the Lakewood Police Department and the Los Angeles Sheriff's Department are abusing the basic principle of privacy, the right to be let alone, which most people say as left alone."

"How so?" asked Olivia.

"Well, I'm no legal scholar, but it seems to me that with all of this fancy technology, it makes it virtually impossible to be 'let alone.'

Olivia stood up and said, "Nigel, that sounds really good. Can you summarize that down to a couple of paragraphs, so that I can review it with Mr. Camarena? Please."

l blinked at Olivia, "A couple of paragraphs?"

"Yes, keep it simple and tight," Olivia asked. " And, how do we get our hands on that information related to that Carnegie Mellon software?"

"Ok, I will draft a summary statement," l said. "And to get more information on the software, we need to request information through the National Defense Archives in Washington, D.C."

"Carle get going on that information from the Archives, I suspect you will need to make a request through the Federal Privacy Act of 1974," Olivia shouted over her shoulder, heading out the door. "I need to speak with the boss."

CHAPTER 13

Camarena, Chavez, and Rosenberg Office
Los Angeles, California
Late February, 1993

Alphonso listened to Olivia outline the backstory, but he still couldn't get his legal mind around it. It was beyond belief that the use of this technology could reliably identify criminals or suspects through the simple process of matching photographs with mugshots. But to get clarification, Alphonso needed to hear it from Nigel himself.

"Come in, Nigel," Alphonso said to me. "Thanks for coming at such late notice."

"Err, you're welcome, sir," I said guardedly. Trying to remember if I had ever spoken more than a few words with Mr. Camarena before.

"Sit, sit. Don't be afraid," the boss chided. "Olivia has spoken very highly of you and tried to explain your thoughts about our defense on the Los Angeles Sheriff's case. But, quite frankly, I need help and would like you to walk me through it."

I looked at Olivia, who nodded in agreement.

"Sit down, Nigel," she said. "Give Mr. Camarena the presentation that you gave me and Carle last week. And, talk a little about the concept of ownership."

After the rebuke from last week, I hadn't really thought much more about the ownership concept. But I did have a few general ideas I could throw out for consideration.

Clearing my throat, I launched into the four-point summary that I had outlined for Olivia and Carle the previous week.

"By linking the development of the imaging software program through DARPA and Carnegie Mellon University, we can suggest that the Lakewood Police Department and the Los Angeles Sheriff's Department are over-reaching the process of surveillance under the Fourth amendment," l said. "Moreover, we can also suggest that they are violating our defendant's Fifth amendment rights."

"How so?" asked Alphonso.

I said,

"Physical form has always intrigued man and woman. Going back in time, we can see through cave paintings to portraiture, how we have tried to vision ourselves in some form. From the rudimentary cave paintings in France to the more highly refined sculptures of the Romans, there has been some form of documenting our existence.

"You can see the learning curve in the process by viewing the rigid, lifeless sculptures of the Egyptians and then trace improvement in skill and understanding through Grecian artefacts ending with the many fine examples in Roman history."

"Yes, that is all fine, and I appreciate the history lesson," said Alphonso, "but what is the connection with the fifth amendment?"

"Okay, just think if every citizen was forced by the government to make a plaster cast of their face for documenting their existence–a physical form to validate their existence that would be held in some storage vault in the United States," I provided.

"That would be preposterous. No one would do that," said Alphonso.

"Well, you are correct," l commented. "But that's basically what people do every day when they get their driver's license. Every driver gives their state's Department of Motor Vehicles tacit approval to store and maintain their likeness. I checked, and there are no controls for who can access and use that information."

I continued, "What we need to demonstrate to the court is that the request to match a composite drawing to a database of any sort, whether from a DMV database or a high school yearbook, violates the basic concept of due process."

"Oh, I get it," Alphonso said out loud. "There was no *a priori* approval to use said photograph for any other purpose. And, to do so now, violates the process of self-incrimination."

"Exactly," I said. "We are not going to be very popular allowing these boys to escape culpability in this case, but we just may very well help shape privacy and anonymity rights for decades to come."

"Well done, Nigel," Alphonso said approvingly. "Olivia, you work out the fine tuning of the legal statutes involved, and let's get this over to opposing counsel right away."

"And, have Carle look into case law regarding First and Fifth Amendment rights. I seem to recall some important cases from the early 1900's."

Olivia walked out of Alphonso's office. This case was starting to take shape with a direction that she would never have thought of in a million years. The input from Nigel was impressive for an intern. It was clear he had the outside-the-box thinking required of such case work. Moreover, it was clear that his understanding of technology was going to be an asset in this case.

Olivia noticed Nigel wasn't in the room when she returned, but Carle was sitting at his desk.

"Where's Nigel?" she asked.

"Oh, he was going over to the computer science department at USC to learn more about the mathematics behind the Carnegie Mellon software system."

"Oh, that sounds useful," she said. "Carle, Mr. Camarena wants you to look into all case law pertaining to the first and fifth amendments. Anything to do with anonymity."

"He mentioned something about a case from the early 1900s," Olivia said.

Carle looked up from his desk with the newspaper spread out to the Los Angeles Time sports section. The Rams were having another terrible year, and there was a rumor going around that they were going to move.

"I can't believe the Rams are thinking about leaving town," Carle sighed. "They are such a big part of this community. It will be a major loss."

Olivia looked at Carle wondering if he heard anything she said. "Carle, it's just a football team. The people of LA will get over it," she commented. "But Mr. Camarena won't get over you not moving on his request."

"Okay, okay," Carle lamented. "I heard what you said, 'early 1900's.' I will look to see what I can find in the Lexis system."

Olivia smiled and walked over to her desk. "Maybe with the Rams gone, we can finally get a professional tennis team in LA," she chuckled.

Carle blanched at the thought. "Yeah, right."

CHAPTER 14

Camarena, Chavez, and Rosenberg Office
Los Angeles, California
Early March, 1993

Waiting for the Lexis system to finish his search on first amendment rights, Carle reflected on how invaluable his relationship with Alphonso has been since the first day they met.

Carle was finishing up his second year at Southwestern Law school when Alphonso came to present a lecture on the history of Latino civil rights in California. It was an engaging and emotional talk that had students and faculty alike mesmerized and in awe.

To say that Alphonso had a way with words was an understatement, but what really made people and jurors take notice was the confidence and clarity attached with every word and phrase. It was almost evangelical.

Alphonso talked about the challenges of Latinos in all industries, not just agriculture. He painted a picture of hardworking people striving for a better life under the most difficult of circumstances. Cesar Chavez was considered the de facto leader of the Latino rights movement, but Alphonso made it clear that there were hundreds, even thousands, of unknown leaders that helped move the movement forward.

Carle noticed that the search had been completed. *I'll be damned,* Carle thought to himself.

Mr. Camarena was right about a relevant privacy case from the early 1900's. In fact, it was from the 1890's and was written by Samuel Warren and Louis Brandeis in response to recent sensationalist newspaper articles. Carle pulled up the First Amendment from the Lexis system:

"Congress shall make no law respecting an establishment of religion, or prohibiting the free exercise thereof; or abridging the freedom of speech, or of the press; or the right of the people peaceably to assemble, and to petition the Government for a redress of grievances."

Most people remember the First Amendment as 'freedom of speech' from their government class in the 10th grade. But, it has much broader powers than what most people think. In fact, one had to think of the context of the founding fathers as they gathered in Philadelphia to write down these requirements. After years of tyranny from the British Empire and the sovereign King of England, the ability to assemble without fear or to speak without reprisal rang true for the signers of the Declaration of Independence.

Carle read the microfiche copy of the 1890 Harvard Law Review article by Warren and Brandeis,

"Instantaneous photographs and newspaper enterprise have invaded the sacred precincts of private and domestic life; and numerous mechanical devices threaten to make good the prediction that 'what is whispered in the closet shall be proclaimed from the house-tops."

Carle was surprised to learn that what 'invaded the sacred precincts' in those days was instant photography conceived by George Eastman. It was the development of a new dry, flexible film for his user-friendly Kodak camera that made this invasion possible. Thinking of the current worries about newspaper gossip and paparazzi, Carle found it interesting that these same concerns were shared 100 years prior.

One key element from the Warren and Brandeis paper stuck out to Carle. It was a case from 1888 regarding Mrs. Pollard and the use of her unapproved likeness on a Christmas card by the Photographic Company. In the proceedings, Mrs. Pollard charged that she had not given permission for the use of her photograph and therefore was seeking to sue for damages to her good reputation.

The plaintiffs' attorney had taken the position that "A person has no property in his own feature."

Luckily for Mrs. Pollard, the court agreed that the company had breached the contract regarding confidentiality and breach of trust, awarding damages to the defendant. What remained unanswered in the final decision proceedings was the position on ownership rights of feature or face.

Carle sketched out some notes on his legal pad, thinking about the Warren and Brandeis article some more. In their article, Sam Warren and Lou Brandeis did not so much address the concept of ownership, but more so the basic tenets for harm and the protection through the right of common law.

Looking further into common law, Carle pulled a reference text from the firm's legal library to gain a better understanding,

"Common law: a judicial system established through customs and precedent; no law should be commended that differed from what a "commoner" would expect from his peers."

The more Carle learned about the Warren and Brandeis article and follow-up court filings pertaining to common law and privacy, the more he contemplated a possible legal position of the firm for the Lakewood case.

Amazingly, Brandeis was instrumental in another important case regarding privacy in the case of Olmstead v United States in 1928 as a Supreme Court Justice. This case revolved around new technology that was impinging on personal privacy at the time. In particular, the development of the telephone and the use of wiretapping for the collection of information against the defendant, Mr. Olmstead.

Justice Brandeis argued that the defendant had every right to believe that his conversations within the confines of his home, whether in person or on the telephone, were indeed personal and private. Sadly, the court decision was 5-4 in favor of the United States allowing for the use of wiretapping for the purpose of information regardless of morality or ethics.

The Justices made it clear that wiretapping did not violate the Fourth or Fifth Amendment rights of Mr. Olmstead. A position that would stand until it was overturned in 1967 with Katz v United States. Carle continued to read the Olmstead case and realized the issue of privacy had been of concern far longer than he had understood. One passage from the Olmstead case stood out to Carle, and that was written by Justice Brandeis:

"The progress of science in furnishing the Government with means of espionage is not likely to stop with wire-tapping. Ways may someday be developed by which the Government, without removing papers from secret drawers, can reproduce them in court, and by which it will be enabled to expose to a jury the most intimate occurrences of the home."

Justice Brandeis further argued that the "right to be let alone" was the most important right available to mankind. Carle agreed with Justice Brandeis, reflecting on his own desire to be left alone. Being alone–that was the feeling he relished while drifting on his surfboard waiting for the next wave.

Picking up his phone, he dialed Olivia's extension, "Olivia, you got a minute?" Carle said. "You won't believe the information I found on privacy and common law."

PART SIX

CHAPTER 15

Austin-Bergstrom International Airport
Austin, Texas
March 13, 2021

His flight from Los Angeles had been delayed by about two hours because of the new travel requirements put in place for the coronavirus pandemic. It seems one of the thermal scan devices suggested that everyone had a fever. Not good!

After about the fifth passenger, TSA finally got the idea that something was wrong. Luckily, Carle had already cleared the area, but he heard later that anyone nearby had to be re-scanned, which is the reason why about half of the plane is not on board when it was time to push away from the gate.

He remembered how crazy things got with airport screening right after 9-11. That was a piece of cake compared to this cluster. The workload of the understaffed TSA has increased two-fold with the added requirement of a thermal face scan along with the new immunity passport verification process.

Carle steps towards Carousel 3 at baggage claim.

"Excuse, me sir. Could you get my bag? Please. It seems trapped on top of those other bags."

Carle looks over at the voice. A middle-aged woman dressed in a casual sundress and sandals. Nice looking. Long black hair pulled off to the side. Light caramel skin with big brown eyes looking over a colorful scarf with yellow and orange hues.

He thought, finally a person expressing a little bit of individuality. He got so tired of those standard green hospital masks that most people wear.

He got a feeling that he has seen her before, or at least those beautiful brown eyes, but he couldn't place it. "No problem," he says reaching over to pull the bag off the carousel. "Here ya go! Do you need any help?"

"No, thanks. I got a baggage guy coming, and he'll help me to the Uber station. I don't want to trouble you anymore," she comments, looking down trying to avoid eye contact.

It would be no problem at all, Carle thought. An older baggage attendant pushing a luggage cart shows up, just about the time Carle was going to ask for her name.

"What is…," Carle says, noticing that the lady has moved on, talking with the attendant.

"Okay, then. Well, enjoy Austin," he says over his shoulder.

Surprisingly, Brown Eyes heard his faint comment. "You, too!" she says looking back at him with a little more interest.

He turned and gives her a little wave. If only I had the time he thought. But he had a lot to do tonight before his meeting with the General tomorrow. And, he needed to be well rested.

Sitting on the edge of the bed trying to wake up, I reflect on how life can throw you a curve when you least expect it.

Bernadette and I had been having an on-again, off-again relationship during the first month of my employment at Face Value. We had been enjoying our time together, not getting caught up in the drama of a new relationship.

It was about mid-February when she came to me crying after learning that her father had been involved in an accident near his home in Bremerton, Washington. He had retired from the US Navy and was living nearby to be close to his friends and the Naval hospital. It was classified as a hit-and-run by the police, but witnesses swore that it seemed more deliberate. Several claimed that they saw a blonde woman head directly for Bernadette's father in the crosswalk and then drove away.

I encouraged Bernadette to take time off and attend to his recovery. I even offered to fly up there and help her settle his affairs. But she refused. She said she would go up on her own and would return as soon as possible. I told her to take her time to grieve and remember her father.

Several weeks later, we all learned that Bernadette's father eventually died from his injuries. It was a sad day for all of us at Face Value and for me. Well, that was until Clare surprised me one day with an invitation to lunch, a lunch that ended with a little dessert for two. And, by the time Bernadette came back to work in early March, Clare had become a stable fixture in my life.

"What're you thinking about, cutie?" Clare moans.

"Oh, nothing. Just thinking about the day ahead," I say standing on my way to the bathroom. "I need to shower. You want me to get you anything?"

"Nope, I just want to lay here a little more," Clare coos.

"Does my lady wish for another shag?" I say in my best Austin Powers voice.

Looking at me, Clare says, "No thanks! And besides, I don't think mini-me is up to the task."

Laughing, she rolls over and buries her head into the pillow. *Funny!*

Stepping into the shower, I began to review the day's schedule at the SXSW Festival. Given all that has happened over the past year with the coronavirus outbreak, the SXSW event is going to be a little different this year. After being cancelled in 2020, the organizers felt that perhaps it is time to get back to its roots.

With that in mind, the event organizers put together a smaller event featuring fewer musical groups but more symposiums on life after COVID-19. The concept of work from home exploded around the world after the lockdown, leading to an increased interest in data center security and the use of artificial intelligence for predicting coronavirus outbreaks.

The one topic that is of most interest to Face Value and me is the trend to ban face recognition technology in public spaces. Most of the major technology firms have instituted a wait-and-see approach on how to best use face recognition given its inherent bias with women and people of color. However, without the use of face recognition software, law enforcement is at a serious disadvantage when it comes to criminal organizations. So, I was extremely interested in the two panels presenting information as to the pros and cons of FR technology in today's world.

Lathering up in the shower, I have to remind myself that the main conference event starts at 9 AM featuring scientific celebrity, Dr. Anthony Fauci, of the National Institute of Allergy and Infectious Disease. After helping the world navigate through the coronavirus pandemic, Dr. Fauci finds himself the celebrity *du jour* on the world stage of radio and television.

Dr. Fauci is going to brief the attendees on the current state of a COVID-19 vaccine. The fact that a vaccine had not been developed is making it difficult to control outbreaks throughout the country and around the world. In fact, most of the world have already gone through a second wave last fall and the likelihood for a third wave this spring is pretty much a given.

Anthony, as he likes to be called in these settings, is going to provide a short chronology of the coronavirus pandemic and then discuss the current thinking on how the United States could "win the war." This is a phrase the President has started to use last summer when it looked like the coronavirus had been beaten. But as any epidemiologist knows, rarely do we ever win against a virus.

I was hoping to hear some good news for a change and perhaps get some insights on when the use of face coverings would be relaxed. While their use helped keep me employed, for the most part they were a pain in the ass. There were enough criminals sneaking around without having to worry about ordinary citizens being considered suspects because of their face mask usage.

After the Fauci talk, there were a couple of smaller events related to thermal scan integration with face recognition software and the use of ear canal thermometry instead of the lower quality thermal scanners being manufactured out of China. These cheap hand-held thermal scanners were not overly sensitive and tended to produce erroneous false positives, resulting in more work for the human screeners.

However, what really got me excited is the talk about face recognition and personal privacy. A topic that was near and dear to me. When I first saw the program webpage, it was her picture that caught my attention. Olivia Vasquez, my friend, and mentor from the law firm of Camarena, Chavez and Rosenburg.

After my shower and while getting dressed, Clare and I discuss schedules. She is going back to the Domain for more shopping but agrees to meet me later in the afternoon for drinks at the hotel lounge, hopefully, followed by dinner with Olivia Vazquez.

"Hopefully, she will remember me," I say.

Clare mumbles something from under the pillow.

"What?" I didn't hear you, poking my head around the bathroom door.

Clare threw the pillow off the bed and sat up. Still naked. Her breasts firm and bountiful, belying her age.

"How could she not remember you?" she laments. "Didn't you guys work together for several years?"

"Well, yes, but you never know. People forget," I shrug.

CHAPTER 16

Austin Hilton Hotel
Austin, Texas
March 13, 2021

South by Southwest is the premiere venue for trends in all thing's media with a little bit of technology thrown in. The idea originated in early 1986, when a bunch of local musical types gathered to talk about shared interests. It became evident that there was a strong interest in more than music and by October, the group had formulated a plan.

Why Austin? You might hear different stories around town, from the taco carts along North Lamar Boulevard to the BBQ joints around East 4th Street. But the truth is no one really knows. It just happened. The music scene was starting to take hold in the clubs along the old parts of town, east of the capitol building, known as East Austin. From honky-tonk bars that served blue-collar workers nearby to the college kids and professors from the University, this part of Austin was fast becoming as a place to be and be seen.

Why SXSW started in Austin isn't quite clear, but it was possibly the focus on technology at the University of Texas, Austin in the late 1950's. But when talking with the locals, some might say what really turned Austin into the town it is today, can be traced to a dorm room at the University of Texas. A room occupied by a student more interested in pre-med at the time, but with a knack for computers and self-promotion. That student was Michael Dell. From that dorm room sprung the seed for PC's Limited and the beginning of the direct-to-consumer trend in home computers.

"See you later tonight," I shout to Clare, closing the door behind me.

Moving quickly down the hallway, I jump into the elevator just as the doors start to close.

"Phew, didn't think I was going to make that," I chuckle, looking around at my companions. Not a peep. Some are looking at their phones, one lady is reading the Wall Street Journal, and a couple seem to be arguing about drinking too much last night. And, none of them are wearing face coverings. Interesting!

"You better not embarrass me tonight," says a tall African American woman. "I am not going to watch you make a fool of yourself in front of my colleagues again."

"But, sugar. I didn't mean…"

"Don't you *sugar* me, Reggie," the lady says with a scowl. "It has taken me 6 years to become CEO, and I am not about to let you bring me down."

Sugar glares at a man who I assume is her husband, "You keep that shit up, and I will send your sorry ass back to Detroit."

Boom. A punch to the gut. Naturally, just when the conversation starts to get juicy, the elevator door chimes. "Second floor, mezzanine level."

Sugar steps forward and heads out the elevator, looking back at Reggie, "You fix this by the time I finish my lecture, or we are done!"

Gulp. Awkwardly our eyes meet. Reggie shrugs his shoulders and tilts his head back all cool like.

"She don't mean that, she my baby," he boasts, I think more trying to convince himself than the others in the elevator.

The chime rings. "First floor, hotel lobby."

Reggie rushes past me. Evidently, the thought of going back to Detroit was on his mind.

The chime rings, "Elevator closing, going up."

l had a passing thought about the elevator voice. *Blonde or Brunette.*

"Excuse me, sir. Are you going to get out?" says a nervous looking, 30-something tech bro.

"Oh, yes. Sorry," l respond, looking around to see who had spoken.

Noticing that it was just the two of us, I wink. "I was just trying to imagine the woman behind that voice. What do you think, blonde or brunette?"

Tech bro looks at me suspiciously, "I don't really think we should be talking about that, sir," he says adjusting his Patagonia vest. "It seems a bit chauvinistic."

"Yeah, you're right. Well, have a good day," l say, stepping around the nerd, jetting out of the elevator and toward that opening session. Idiot!

I take a quick right and slam right into the back of a woman. She stumbles forward, but catches herself, looking back to see what *idiot* ran into her.

"I am so sorry," I begin to say, but soon realize that it is her.

"Olivia," I stammer. "Olivia Vazquez."

The lady moves aside to let other people pass, looking at me, a bit cautious trying to find something in her memory that says *she knows this guy.*

"Hello, I'm sorry," a nervous look on her face. "Do we know each other?"

"It's me, Nigel Grant." Blank face. "…from Los Angeles and CCR!"

Her brain is still stuck in neutral, but eventually, a glimmer of light comes on. "Oh, my God! Yes, Nigel. How are you? What are you doing here?" her enthusiasm gaining momentum as she remembers the face and the place.

"I'm here on a work assignment," I say. "But I plan on attending your session later this afternoon."

Olivia gathers her briefcase and purse from the floor.

"Can we get together after your talk?" I ask.

"Yes, of course. I would love to catch up. Hang around after my talk and once I'm done chatting with the attendees, we can go get coffee or a drink," she shouted, turning away, rushing towards the exit.

CHAPTER 17

Austin Hilton Hotel
March 13, 2021

"**O**kay, see you later tonight!" Nigel shouts closing the hotel room door.

Clare didn't waste any time. She had agreed with Nigel to meet him later for dinner with that attorney broad. But she has something important that needs to be done, first.

And, for this she needs a different look. It is a good thing that Nigel is not interested in her daily movements. He is clueless on a lot of things that she does, which makes it so much easier for her to fulfill her destiny.

Looking in the mirror, she smiles. Acknowledging her firm breasts and thin waistline, she is proud that men still look at her. *Girl, not bad for 45 years,* she whispers under her breath. Her good fortune is genetics and all that hard work she does at the gym. But, still. She is pushing the age boundary in a business that doesn't forgive or forget.

Opening her make-up bag, she clicks open the secret compartment on the bottom, revealing a blonde wig and a mishmash of hair bows, clips, and scrunchies. *Who came up with the name, scrunchy?* she thought.

Munchy, crunchy. Oh my god, she thought to herself, I sound just like Nigel when he goes off on one of his tangents. She rolls her eyes and slides the blonde wig over her short, coal black hair.

Nigel pleads for her to grow it long, but that makes it difficult when she needs to slip on wigs or caps or hats. She just tells him that long hair makes her look old. A lame excuse for sure, but he accepts it without suspicion.

A little mascara, blue-green eyeshadow, and dark red lipstick seal the deal. This is not the time to hide behind a face covering she thought. It is time to be bold.

"My name is Chanel," she says in her native French accent. "Hello, Mr. Harper. The General has changed our meeting place. We now go to hotel, not convention center."

She rehearses it repeatedly. The General had sent her an encrypted text outlining his plan. They were to meet at the hotel and not the convention center.

The General did not want Carle encountering Nigel or Olivia too soon. He needs time to get Carle to understand the situation, to get him to see that it is the only way they can get answers.

Clare slid on her black stretch pants, ankle boots, and a sexy black and silver belt. The short crop-top she bought at Nordstrom Rack for $15 is perfect. It is form-fitting but gives her just enough coverage to not be obscene. A simple bomber-style jacket is the finishing touch.

A quick look in the full-length mirror on the bathroom door, a slight adjustment of the blonde wig, and she is off. With a shoulder bag and the Glock 43 in tow, she is ready to meet the day.

The Glock 43 is perfect for her purpose, small enough for easy concealment but with a bang. The Glock 42 is smaller, but the 380 ammo doesn't give quite the punch like the 9 mm from the 43. And, in her business, she needs as much as she can muster.

Slipping out of the hotel room without notice, Clare moves down the hallway towards destiny.

PART SEVEN

CHAPTER 18

Los Angeles, California
September 8, 1972

Saul Rosenberg arrived in Los Angeles just days after the Palestinians took eleven Israeli Olympic athletes' hostage in Munich, Germany on September 5th in 1972. The tragedy that later unfolded at the Munich airport consumed the International news at a time when television was the primary communication medium of the day. Long before the impact of Twitter or Facebook on daily life.

There was concern about further violence against Jews around the world. This concern spread through the Jewish neighborhoods located throughout Los Angeles. And, given the tenuous race relations in Southern California, there was some worry that some of the Hispanic and Black gangs would use it as an opportunity to further their reach into other communities.

Naturally, Saul had no idea about the sorry state of race relations in Los Angeles, but it would soon be the opportunity of a lifetime.

Driving along Century Boulevard from the Los Angeles airport in his Uncle Maury's convertible Mustang, Saul was amazed that the California scenery was just like the pictures he saw in the *Ladies Home Journal* at the dentist's office.

His Uncle Maury lived in Studio City, California, just over the Santa Monica mountains in the San Fernando Valley. It wasn't Los Angeles or anything, but for Maury it afforded him easy access into Hollywood, and it was cheap.

"Saul, when I came through the Long Beach port after World War II, and I looked around, all I could see was sunshine and dames," Maury told him over the phone. "There was no way I was going back to the cold winters of Connecticut."

From what Saul could see heading east on Santa Monica Boulevard, he thought that made a lot of sense.

Maury was from his mom's side of the family, and Saul didn't know him very well. But, the offer of free room and board and help finding a job, made it hard to say no!

During the war, Uncle Maury was in procurement for the U.S. Navy. From ships to shitters, Mo, as he was called, could purchase and at times borrow just about anything.

"There isn't much difference between procuring and borrowing something for the U.S. government," Maury chuckled over lunch at his favorite deli, Art's on Ventura Boulevard in Studio City.

Art's was a favorite haunt of the local Jewish community since the late 1950's. If you wanted a good smear of cream cheese and lox on an everything bagel, Art's was the place to go. Saul sat in the corner of the booth, facing the main dining area. From what he could see, Art's had the look of a business that was not going to be around long.

The booths were torn and ragged, the floors were dirty, some with red carpet and some with white linoleum. The walls needed a good painting, and the windows were filthy.

"Uncle Maury, is it okay to eat here? It seems a bit dirty," Saul shared a look around.

"Whaddya talking about?" Maury exclaimed, waving his hands and arms around in the air. "This all around is *charm*. Don't let appearances fool you."

Saul picked up his water glass, spying what appeared to be ketchup on the rim.

"Hey, sometimes you get a little extra bonus, free of charge." Maury grinned.

With that Maury pulled out a slip of paper from his jacket pocket. "Now, here are a few names I was able to *procure* from Francine at the studio," Maury winked.

"Francine is all legs and lips like cherries," Maury whistled. "I've been trying to get her out for drinks for years. But, nothin.'"

Maury unfolded the paper and pointed to a few names. "This guy at Warner Brothers was in the Navy, and I have been known to procure a few things for him every now and then. He likes Jews, and I think he might consider hiring you."

"What line of work are you in again?" Saul questioned.

"Procurement," Maury smiled. "Most of them are legal, but a guy's gotta make a living, so every now and then I help people find special things that might be questionable in terms of the law."

"Know what I'm saying, kid?" With that *mea culpa*, Maury looked down at the slip of paper.

"Come to think of it, I would try this place first," Maury said pointing to a name on the list. "I don't know the guy personally, but Francine says he is a *mentsch*," Maury said pointing over his shoulder. "In fact, it is just around the corner on Lankershim Boulevard."

Saul looks where Uncle Maury was pointing. "Okay, what kind of business is it?" Saul asked.

"It's a recording studio, you know for rock bands," Maury shrugged. "Not my cup of tea, but this guy, Marvin, seems to bring in the shekels and the babes."

With that news, Saul's career path was set in motion.

Not too far away, Alphonso Camarena was getting used to living back in the States after serving his time in the U.S. Marines Corps. The world of a civilian was a little different than what Alphonso was expecting when he was discharged from the Corps in July.

The adulation and respect shown the men and women who fought during World War II was absent for the thousands of soldiers returning from Vietnam in 1972. For many Americans, these soldiers sold out to the "Man," fighting a senseless war instead of staying home and fighting for civil rights. The disdain and anger were most notable in young adults and teens, many who had the privilege of birth to not serve.

The anti-war protests and slurs yelled his way did not really bother Alphonso. He believed in the Corps and the brotherhood. If the deaths and bombings changed the world, so be it. All Alphonso knew was that staying in East LA meant certain death while Vietnam offered him better odds. In the end, the Corps more than likely saved his life.

Alphonso went back home upon discharge from the Marines. East LA had become ground zero for the gang wars between the Blacks and the Hispanics. It was a battle for dominance and territory. He begged his parent's countless times to move with him away from the crime and violence. But they always said East LA was their place, and they would leave when the good Lord called them home.

Sadly, Alphonso got to see them get their wish on the day he was accepted into Whittier College, just down the 60 Freeway. They were sitting out on the porch, like they did most days, when a gang ambush happened directly in front of their home. When it was all over, the Los Angeles Sheriff's office determined that his parents had been killed by stray bullets between the rival gangs.

Naturally, people would understand if Alphonso wanted to extract vengeance on the gang members. But Alphonso had learned in the Marines Corps that violence only brought more violence, and what purpose would that serve?

So, with the little money he got from selling his parents' house and the money he got from the G.I. Bill, Alphonso moved to Whittier and to a new life. It was the death of his parents that brought a sense of urgency to complete college as quickly as possible. The G.I. Bill paid for college and a nice apartment near the Whittier College campus. Going to school was nothing compared to humping a 120-pound shoulder pack through the rice paddies of Vietnam.

He finished his first year with good grades and decided to take an introductory law class over the summer. Professor Hopkins taught introductory law as part of the general pre-law curriculum that Whittier College offered to the students. It was felt that focusing and shaping the students' interest early gave them an advantage when applying to the predominantly Caucasian law schools in Southern California.

Professor Hopkins took an interest in the young Marine Corps veteran. "Did the people who killed your parents ever get charged?" he asked Alphonso one day after class.

Alphonso hadn't really thought about his parents in a couple of months and didn't quite know how to respond. "I don't think so," Alphonso admitted. " Last I heard; the cops didn't have enough evidence to convict."

"Didn't you tell me once that they were shot on their patio, right in front of some neighbors?" Hopkins said.

"Yeah, they were all outside when it happened. My parents were just the unlucky ones to get caught in the cross-fire," Alphonso sighed. "People said it happened so fast, they couldn't remember the car or the faces. But I think they were scared!"

"Do you blame them?" Hopkins asked Alphonso. "Like our discussion today on the Fifth Amendment, they have the right to protect themselves from self-incrimination in a court of law, something they might say could be used against them."

"No, I don't blame them. I blame the system," Alphonso said.

"But, more importantly, they also have the right to protect themselves from neighborhood retaliation," Professor Hopkins reviewed. "In this case, your neighbors are stuck between helping to serve justice at the expense of their own life."

Hopkins commented as he pointed to the picture of Lady Justice on Alphonso's textbook.

"It is foolhardy to think that anyone can be impartial, so we must rely upon the balance of evidence presented in a court of law. Those that can best communicate the merits for acquittal or conviction will win every time, whether we agree or not."

Before turning away, Alphonso heard one more thing from the Professor, "and that, Mr. Camarena, is what the legal profession is all about. Good day!"

With those words, Alphonso's desire to represent the poor, the disadvantaged, and the immigrant grew stronger. A desire that would eventually lead him to Saul Rosenberg and the chance to make a difference.

CHAPTER 19

Southern France, 1972

Half-way around the world, change was spreading across Europe in the 1970s, most notably in France. The death of the great French military hero and statesmen Charles de Gaulle threw the young Fifth Republic into turmoil.

de Gaulle led the interim French government between 1944 to 1946 just after the German military had been defeated. It had become quite evident that the former German-occupied country lacked a cohesive system of government to manage the post-war resurgence. Thankfully, de Gaulle stepped in to help provide structure and guidance with the development for a presidential system of government leading to what became the Fourth Republic. Sadly, once de Gaulle stepped down, this new republic soon resembled the prior corrupt republic, eventually losing favor with the French citizens. While the Fourth Republic prospered economically, it failed miserably in the management of many social causes important to the French citizens.

While the French were apathetic on many issues, the most pressing at the time was the French involvement in the Indochina war against communism and the conflict in Algeria.

Ultimately, the military coup in Algeria all but ended the Fourth Republic requiring Charles de Gaulle to once again step in and bring order to a dysfunctional country.

General de Gaulle used his reputation and influence to propose a new constitutional system and was eventually selected to govern the new Fifth Republic as President from 1958 until his death in 1970. The election of Georges Pompidou in 1970 did not seem to suppress the chaos and turmoil that soon followed. Turmoil fueled by the Arab Oil Embargo beginning in 1972 lead to increased energy prices, a failing economy, and slowly rising unemployment. France was already reeling from its lost status in the world order, and the French people were becoming disenchanted with the post-war economic plan developed and guided by the academic and government elites.

Eve Marie Rahmani was one of the disenchanted. She was Algerian by birth and considered one of the *pied noir* immigrants who entered France in the late 1960's as part of the French-Algerian conflict. Young Eve Marie was learning that the France of her dreams was not what she experienced every day.

Jacques, her father, had remained in Algeria after the military coup in 1958. He felt that being a 'true' Algerian would allow him status in the newly formed government. But he did have the wisdom to secure safe passage for his wife and Eve Marie, to the French continent in 1960. They eventually learned that he did not last exceptionally long within the new regime, being executed as a conspirator of the French government in 1963.

Eve Marie and her mother eventually settled in the southern port of Marseille in 1965. The French government did not really feel comfortable helping the *pied noir* people, but the sins of post-colonial rule forced them to accept them, albeit reluctantly. Well, at least until it became clear that these newly arrived French citizens would start to take jobs away from the 'real' French people. Then, the *pied noir* was deemed unworthy of their French citizenship, and assistance by the Pompidou government soon disappeared.

With a young son and daughter, Eve Marie was learning that survival often meant unpleasant choices including the companionship of men. These men helped pay for the food and clothes on their backs, asking little in return. But that is not how Eve Marie's mother saw it, and she eventually took Clare Marie and Charles to live with friends in Perpignan.

For Charles, the plan went well. And, when Eve learned that sweet, innocent Clare had been sent to live and study with the Poor Clares at the St. Clare Monastery, it seemed ordained. God had directed Eve to name her daughter Clare, and in return, Clare was to serve God the almighty.

Eve Marie felt relieved that Clare would be safe and educated. She felt comfort knowing that Clare would serve God and God only.

The teaching of God often inspired Clare to seek clarity. For to read and hear the spoken word of God often took a circuitous path. And, for Clare, that did not often reconcile with what she felt inside.

"Why must we believe in God?" she questioned Sister Mary Joseph one summer day in her thirteenth year.

"Because God is all around us. He guides the Sun and the Moon. He brings the rain and the harvest," said Sister Mary Joseph.

"I do not see him," said Clare. "Does he not know that I am looking for him?"

"He knows that you are looking for him, but he asks that you be patient," Sister Mary said.

"I am patient. And, have we not been patient all these months without rain?" Clare said. "Does God not see that we need rain for nourishment and harvest?"

"You must believe," is all that Sister Mary could say. For Clare that meant the end of another circuitous path of unanswered questions.

"I would believe more if I knew more about God," said Clare. "Is God a man or a woman?"

Making a slight gasp, Sister Mary looked around hoping that the other devout sisters did not hear this question. "God is the Almighty," she said. "And that is the last of this conversation young lady."

Clare still felt that her question had not been answered. "But if Jesus is the son of God," she said. "Doesn't it make sense that God would look like Jesus?"

Sister Mary Joseph threw up her hands in defeat. "You exasperate me, Clare of Marseille! Now run along and say your prayers before supper."

"Thank you, Sister Mary Joseph," said Clare turning towards the chapel. Clare wondered more about God. In her mind, her conviction would be strengthened if his likeness could be verified once and for all. Kneeling in the chapel looking at the face of Jesus of Nazareth high atop the altar, Clare had a momentous thought. Perhaps she could prove it a different way.

CHAPTER 20

That face. Saul knew he had seen that face before, but he just couldn't place it. Since working for the record company, he had seen a lot of famous singers and composers come through the door. But this guy just seemed a little peculiar, not that Saul hadn't seen his share of *peculiar* since living in the Valley for the past seven years.

Saul waited until the guy walked out of the door before he asked Estelle his name.

"That's Syd. He is in one of those punk bands from London," Estelle said. "He may look a little different, but he is a sweetheart–never forgets to bring me bagels from Gelman's when he is in town."

Saul wasn't sure about that, but if Estelle liked him then he must be a good guy. Rarely had he found her judgment in question. In fact, she was his go-to person for all information circulating around Hollywood and Los Angeles. As a matter of fact, Estelle had connections throughout Southern California.

"What? Estelle, I didn't hear you," Saul said coming out of his daydream.

"Don't forget you have an appointment with Ira Gelman and one of his clients today," Estelle said.

"Yeah, got it on my calendar. What's it about again?" Saul asked.

"Ira wants you to consider representing one of his clients," she said. "Apparently, he was roughed up by a couple of police officers over on Wilshire for being Jewish."

"Holy crap, Estelle," Saul said. "Will we ever move on from the persecution?!"

Later in the afternoon, Ira and his client, David, were sitting in his office.

"Saul, you gotta do better than that. Isn't it time we put all of this bigotry behind us?" Ira said.

Saul looked at Ira and then at David. He had to admit that David looked like he had the shit beaten out of him, but the particulars of the circumstances seemed just a little off the mark.

"Okay, let's go through this one more time," Saul said. "Now David, explain to me again how it was you came upon these officers?"

"Like I said, I had a dinner meeting with my manager at the Beverly Wilshire until about 11 PM. We had a few drinks in the bar, and I headed home around midnight," David explained. "I live over by LACMA and as I was driving through the intersection at San Vicente Boulevard, the cops pull out of the liquor store on the corner with their lights flashing."

"Saul, what does it matter? Look what they did to his face," Ira pleaded. "He makes his living off them dimples."

"Ira, I get it, but we need to consider the procedural circumstances, which the police officers will use for pulling Mr. Dimples over," Saul said.

"David, what kind of car were you driving?" Saul asked.

"I got a sweet looking 1975 Porsche 911," David said proudly.

"Is it possible that you could have been going a little too fast through that intersection?" Saul asked.

"I coulda been going a little fast, but the cops said they pulled me over because one of my taillights was out," David said. "But that was bull shit, because I just had it serviced at the dealer last week."

"And, when they came up to your window, what happened?" Saul asked.

"They asked for my driver's license and insurance papers," David said. "Then, the big one asked me to get out of the car. He told his partner that he smelled a lot of alcohol coming off my breath."

"And?" asked Saul.

"Well, I got out of my car and walked over to the sidewalk. They made me do a sobriety walk and started asking me to count backwards," David said. "Then, the little cop mentioned to the other guy that I was some famous singer known for my dimples."

Saul wrote down a few things on his yellow legal pad. "Okay, so then what happened?" Saul asked.

"The little cop started saying that I must be a fag because of my dimples and started rubbing my crotch. I pushed him away telling him to stop touching me," David said. "Next thing I know the big guy clocks me from the side with his fist and then slams his stick across my face. After that I don't remember anything until I woke up in my car parked in some strip mall along Wilshire."

"By any chance you catch their names or badge numbers?" Saul asked.

"It's all fuzzy, but I seem to remember the little cop calling the other guy, Lewis," David said.

"Umm, that could be first or last name. Anything else?" Saul asked.

"If I had to guess, the little cop was Italian or something like that," David provided.

"So, we got a cop, maybe named Lewis and one guy that may or may not be Italian," Saul said. "Not a lot of information to take to the District Attorney."

"But, Saul, this isn't just an isolated case," Ira offered. "I've heard of a couple of guys getting roughed up over in Santa Monica and in the Valley. The cops around here are outta control."

"Yeah, I've read some of those articles in the Daily," Saul said. "But, Ira, you know I do mostly business contract litigation. This kind of stuff isn't my thing."

"Well, it ought to be your thing for crying out loud," Ira pleaded. "Somebody needs to hold these cops accountable. What good is that fancy law degree from NYU if not to protect our civil rights?"

Saul looked at David one more time, not liking what he saw, especially at the hands of law enforcement. One thing Saul had learned in law school was the tenuous relationship between the police department and the legal industry including those in the local district attorney's office.

"Let me think about it," Saul said. "Estelle will contact you when I'm ready to talk some more."

"Sounds like a plan, Stan," Ira said.

"What about me?" David asked.

"For now, keep a low profile," Saul said. "And, make sure your taillights are working."

The first time Ira made the pitch about civil rights, Saul had no interest. He had a good thing going with the record company and quite frankly was enjoying life. He didn't want to "Rock the Boat Baby," like the song from a few years ago. But, over the past seven months he had gotten frustrated with the large number of reports of excess force by the LAPD. Not so much in the Jewish neighborhoods but in the Black communities of East LA, Compton, and Inglewood.

Besides the policing issue, many of the ethnic communities were now competing against each other for jobs. Saul had heard recently that unionized Black janitors in downtown Los Angeles were being replaced by non-union immigrants from Central America at almost half the wage. And, to top it off, the Asian population was expected to double over the next decade.

Thinking it through, Saul had seen this all before while growing up in Long Island and living in New York City. Without good government controls and community oversight this could end badly for people of color. And, ever the shrewd businessman, Saul thought it might be time to get out of the music business and into the *people* business.

Now what was the name of that impressive Hispanic law student he met at Southwestern College last year? The time might be right for a multi-ethnic law firm in Los Angeles to serve people of color. And, from what he remembered, that kid had the right stuff!

PART EIGHT

CHAPTER 21

Jennifer's parents didn't quite welcome her back with open arms. There was a lot of yelling and screaming about stuff going back decades. Come to find out Jennifer didn't really have all that great of a relationship with her folks. This put a little twist on our move back and our personal relationship.

By the summer of 2010, Jen and I were often at odds about what to do and how to do it. Whether it be weekend chores or paying bills, we were growing apart. And, soon Jennifer began to change, slowly but ever so noticeable. It was the little things, but eventually there became a pattern. Every morning started with brunch, and of course, a Bloody Mary. Every afternoon became 'happy hour'! She would start with wine and then slowly move up the ladder to whiskey, before passing out watching some late-night television program.

It was difficult to understand her change, but I suspected part of it was her inability to get a job. When we moved to Portland, she felt confident and strong. The local girl returned from her adventure to the East Coast, ready to share all her knowledge and experience with the community.

Her education and knowledge were of limited value to the people that lived here now. Oregon and Portland are structured in a hierarchy. If you didn't wear the neon green of the University of Oregon or the black and orange of Oregon State, you were an outsider. But growing up in Portland and going through the Portland City School system had to amount to something. Surely, they would see that Jennifer was one of them. Ready to share what she had learned on her travels.

All she wanted to do was share the wisdom gleamed while traversing the hallowed halls of academia in New England. Not with malice, but to help make Portland a better place. Sadly, her time away was considered awkward, uncomfortable, and uninspiring.

There wasn't much I could do but support her effort, to encourage her not to give up. But it had little effect on her. Her desire, energy, and commitment, slowly fading with every rejection over the course of two years. I had thought getting her involved with gardening would be beneficial, but that didn't last long. And, when I tried to get her parents to help with intervention, they just looked the other way. It became evident soon after arriving in Portland that access to medical marijuana was reasonably easy. And, little did I know, by 2012 Jennifer had become the best customer of the marijuana shop just around the corner.

It all came to a head one day when I tried to get Jen to attend an addiction treatment program offered through the county health services department.

"Fuck you, Nigel," Jennifer spoke, her breath heavy with alcohol and smelling of pot. "I don't need any help."

"But you do need help," I begged. "The Jennifer I know is gone. I want her back."

Jennifer stared at me with glazed eyes, wavering, swaying side to side, and whispering,

"That bitch ain't ever coming back!" before passing out and landing at my feet.

Sitting in the lobby of the Emergency Room at the Milwaukie Hospital, I wondered if I really wanted Jennifer back. Was I just saying that because it was expected or did, I really want her back?

I mean we had been separated for about 8 months now, and I just didn't have that loving feeling. It was 2012, and the fun and excitement of our big move to Portland was waning. Well, at least for me it was.

Evidently, Jennifer had been having a grand time.

"Mr. Grant," I heard from behind.

Startled out of my thoughts I responded, "Yes?"

"Sorry to sneak up on you, but I have information about your wife."

I turned around in the chair to get a better look at whoever was speaking to me, "Hi. I'm Dr. Johnson."

I stood up and looked at what appeared to be a junior high student, braces, and all, wearing a doctor's white lab coat.

"Sorry?" I responded.

"Your wife is Jennifer, correct?" she replied.

"Yes," I said. "I'm Nigel Grant, and we are actually separated."

"Oh, that isn't in our records. You are listed as her primary contact," Dr. Johnson said, trying to decide if she had made an error in talking with me.

"Yes, it is an amicable separation, and we still list each other as primary contacts," I offered.

"Okay," she said relieved. "Let's sit down, and I will review our findings."

Looking around for some privacy, we walked over to a corner near the entrance.

"It appears your wife had a severe reaction due to a combination of alcohol and prescription medicine," the doctor said. "Do you know about any of the medications she is taking?"

I sat there confused. "Not really," I said. "We've been separated for about 8 months, so it could be anything."

"Well, her symptoms seemed to be related more with central nervous system depressants than anything else. Medications for seizures or pain relievers perhaps. There shouldn't be any long-term issues, but I would encourage you to help her get counseling," she said, placing her hand on my shoulder.

"Do you think this was an overdose?" I worried. "Suicide?"

"No, I don't think suicide, but just a miscalculation. It sounds like a lot of things have been going on in her life, so maybe she was just distracted," Dr. Johnson said. "But it would still be a good idea to get her into counseling."

"Oh, that is a relief," I said. "I was worried that I had missed something."

"People can be pretty good at hiding things like this when they need to," the doctor said.

Dr. Johnson stood up. Looking at me she said, "Your wife had a pretty tough day and is probably going to be asleep until morning, so why don't you go home and get some sleep yourself."

She gave me a courteous smile and walked back into the office.

I didn't need sleep, but I didn't feel like staying there. But it might not be a bad idea to go see what Jennifer had been doing around the house.

Standing looking in the medicine cabinet at the Sellwood house, I remembered something Carle said to me about pain relievers one day at work. He had banged up his knee surfing, and I had asked if he was taking any medication.

"Nah, I got some aspirin at home. You gotta be careful with some of those painkillers," he said hobbling over to his desk.

I could see why Jennifer had to go to the emergency room. Evidently, she was trying every painkiller available to see which one worked best: Vicodin, Percocet, OxyContin. And, a few names I had never heard of that contained morphine and fentanyl.

Rummaging around in the kitchen I found countless wine bottles and several empty prescription bottles, not to mention a stack of bills stamped with "Due" in bright red ink and a few letters from collection agencies.

Looking out of the French doors into the backyard I could see the faint tinge of red in the sky. Night had become morning. As I filled an empty shopping bag with all the prescription containers, I knew that the day ahead would be full of pain and sorrow.

Groggy from my lack of sleep, I swung through the Starbucks on Tacoma Avenue on my way back to the hospital. A good cup of dark roast would be welcome. I needed to be on top of my game because I knew there was going to be a battle.

I knew there was no way I was going to get Jen to enroll in an addiction treatment program and getting any support out of her parents was out of the question. They still hadn't warmed up to her since moving back.

But, the biggest battle today was going to be with the hospital. While looking through the stack of bills, I came across a letter from our medical insurance. It appeared that Jennifer had forgotten to make premium payments for three months, and our health insurance policy had been cancelled, which meant I was doubly-fucked–dealing with Jennifer and not having medical insurance.

As I walked into the hospital room, Dr. Johnson was finishing up some paperwork. Wearing a nice knee-length skirt and fashionable top, she looked older than the junior high student from yesterday.

"Well, good morning," she commented as I entered the room. "Did you have as good a night as Jennifer?"

Jennifer looked at me suspiciously.

"Not so much," I said sitting down in the chair in the corner of the room.

"Morning, Jen," I said.

"What's in the bag?" Jennifer asked me.

"Tell me, Doc. How is the patient today?" I inquired. "Will she be able to go home?"

"Possibly. We need to run just a couple more tests," Dr. Johnson said. "I won't really know until later this afternoon."

"Okay," I said. "Can we talk outside about our discussion from yesterday?"

"Why sure," Dr. Johnson replied. Both she and Jennifer looked at me suspiciously. Closing the door behind us with Jennifer staring at us, Dr. Johnson asked, "What's up?"

"Well, I couldn't sleep last night, so I went over to our house, to look around," I said. "And, this is what I found along with a lot of wine bottles."

I opened the bag for her to see. "Oh, my," she said, poking around and pulling out some prescription bottles. "This is quite the collection."

"Yes, I Googled some of the names, and it appears some are opioids," I offered.

"Uh, huh," Dr. Johnson confirmed. Standing next to her, I could smell her perfume and got the sense there was a little electricity flowing between us.

"And, that's not the worst of it," I shared.

"Really?" she said.

"Unfortunately, while rummaging around, I found a letter from our health insurance company canceling our insurance for lack of payment."

Standing in the hallway near the nurses' station, all she could say was "shit!"

"My thought exactly," I said, turning around to head back into Jennifer's room.

CHAPTER 22

Milwaukie Hospital
Milwaukie, Oregon
November 12, 2012

Walking into Jen's hospital room, she asked, "What's going on Nigel?"

"How are you feeling Jen?" I replied. "You gave us all a pretty big scare."

"Don't give me that shit, Nigel," she cursed. "What did you have in that shopping bag?"

"First things first, Jennifer," I said, hoping to set a more formal tone. "We need to talk about a few things before we get to that."

"Like what?" Jen asked, sitting up in the bed, pushing the sheets off her legs.

I could sense she was getting a little bit agitated.

"Just relax," I said. "Nothing that we can't work out."

"Yesterday, when I went to the house to get some new clothes for you, I kind of noticed that it was a mess."

"You went to get me some clothes?" she questioned.

"Um, yeah," I lied.

"Where are they?" she noticed.

"Well, let's just say that a few other things became more important than getting you new clothes," I said.

"Such as?" she asked.

"Well, for one, I came across a bunch of bills that haven't been paid in quite some time," I shared.

"Cash has been a little tight these days," she explained.

"Hmm, but not so tight that you couldn't buy all the wine and beer I saw in the kitchen?"

"Fuck you. I don't need to explain to you," she yelled. "If you remember, we're separated, asshole."

"Yes, you are correct," I said. "We have been separated, but we did agree that we would work to keep our finances together during the process. Which brings up an important problem."

"What?" she said.

"It appears our health insurance has been cancelled," I stated.

She didn't quite say it, but I was pretty sure she had the same thought as Dr. Johnson.

"Yeah, that is going to be a real bummer," I said. "We're going to need to work together on this to work it out."

"I'm sorry Nigel. I've tried so hard to keep it together, but I just can't anymore!" Jen cried out.

I walked over to the bed and clasped her hand. "It's okay, but actually, that is the least of my concerns."

Jennifer stopped crying and looked at me, "The shopping bag?"

"Yes, I found all of the prescription medicine that you had throughout the house. Some pretty nasty stuff, Jen," I said not wanting to be patronizing. "How'd you get all those medications?"

"It started with my dentist when I had that root canal," she said. "He said it would help take the edge off the pain."

"The dentist?" I queried.

"Yes, he said that I could stop after a few days, but I found they made me feel so good, I couldn't stop," she admitted.

"Your dentist gave you all those different prescriptions?" I asked.

"No, I got some from the vet for the dog, and then I found some guy at the pot shop who supplied the rest."

I stood there looking at her. "You took the pills away from Snickerdoodle?" I said. Snickerdoodle was our Labrador Poodle mix that we adopted from the humane society.

"Yes, he didn't need them after a couple of days," she said.

"Yeah, but," I said to no one in particular. "You're taking medications prescribed for a dog."

I guess not having an addiction one doesn't understand the drive for such things. But I eventually learned that animal medications were one of the leading access points for people with opioid addiction.

"Jen, we've got to get you some help," I pleaded. "This has got to stop."

Jennifer looked at me in a way that I hadn't seen in a long time.

"You're right. I've been fooling myself thinking I could handle it," she admitted.

And, right on cue, Dr. Johnson walked through the door followed by an older gentleman who could've been her grandfather.

"Well, look at you two talking," Dr. Johnson said. "Glad to see you guys are getting along and talking things through."

"I want to introduce you to Dr. Jasper," Dr. Johnson nodded. "He is in charge of our counseling program."

"Jennifer, after what your husband, excuse me, Nigel, showed me in the shopping bag, I thought it might be time for you to talk to someone," Dr. Johnson said. "And, there is no one better in Portland than Dr. Jasper."

The lack of sleep and emotion of it all hit me like a brick. Feeling faint I had to sit down and catch my breath.

"Nigel, you okay?" Dr. Jasper said.

"Yes, I'm fine. Just a little tired from not sleeping last night and lack of food," I said. "I think I'll just go home and get some rest."

"I think that's a grand idea. We've got it covered here, Nigel," Dr. Johnson said, pushing me towards the door. "Go home, get a little food, and take a nap."

I stood up still a little wobbly. "You okay, Jen?" I asked.

"It's okay," she replied. "I'll give my parents a call and have them take me home."

I buttoned up my jacket and headed out the door.

"And, Nigel?" Jen said.

I turned to look at her, "Yes?"

"Don't ever fucking sneak into my house again!"

With that cheery goodbye, I stepped into the hall and out of her life with Black Sabbath's *Crazy Train* playing inside my head, remembering that Snickerdoodle hadn't been in the house. *Fuck.*

PART NINE

CHAPTER 23

Camarena, Chavez, and Rosenberg Office
Los Angeles, California
April 19, 1993

It's hard to believe, but basically, you can take a picture of anyone in public without their consent. And, unless you are using it for illegal purposes, you can publish it as well," Carle informed Olivia and me.

"What? That's crazy," l said. "Where does privacy come in?"

"That's a great question. In fact, there is precedence regarding intrusions on a person's right to 'be let alone' from the early work of Warren and Brandeis we talked about last week," Carle said.

"How so?" inquired Olivia.

"Remember, Warren and Brandeis felt that the intrusion by the newspaper and instant camera technologies ran afoul of common decency and the basic right to be left alone."

This legal ruling was used in a famous case brought by Jacqueline Kennedy Onassis against a photographer who was becoming a little too aggressive in his quest for candid photographs of the Onassis family," Carle said. "This was the early 70's, and the paparazzi industry was just beginning."

"Oh, yeah. I remember that case from one of my Pepperdine case review projects," Olivia noted, taking a minute to scan her prodigious legal memory.

"Galella v Onassis, 1973 or 1974," Oliva said. "The courts affirmed that Mr. Galella could take a picture of the Onassis family as part of his First Amendment rights, but his actions were so egregious that they placed a 25-foot restraining order on him. That distance was arbitrarily deemed important for establishing what constitutes "being alone."

"Bravo, Olivia," said Carle. "It was actually 1973, and Jackie Onassis repetitioned again in 1982 because it was shown that Mr. Galella had repeatedly violated the original order."

I looked at Olivia and Carle amazed, "I like all this cool legal stuff, but it sounds like there is no legal basis to prevent the use of the photographs from the yearbooks."

"Yes and no," Carle said. "The parents have no parental right or control of the photographs and their use. So, we can't use that line of reasoning. But we might be able to look at copyright infringement of the yearbook photographs."

"Tell us a little more about that Carle," Olivia asked.

"Okay, here's my idea. All parents give implied consent for any photograph to be used of their child in a school yearbook. But what we are not considering is the ownership of the photographs by whoever took the photo, because they are considered a property right under the Federal Copyright Act of 1976."

Olivia said it first, "So, we make a motion to vacate the legal actions on the grounds that the Los Angeles Sheriff's Department violated copyright protection laws when they scanned the photographs in the Lakewood High School yearbooks?"

Carle nodded his head–affirmative.

"Carle, that is brilliant," Olivia said with a grin. "Find out who published the yearbook."

We stood around thinking about what we had all agreed was a fairly good idea. The silence of our own personal reflection was broken by Olivia's phone.

Olivia picked up the phone on the second ring. "Yes," Olivia said, listening to the voice on the other side. "Okay, we'll be right over." Olivia placed the phone back on the cradle and stared ahead. A perplexed look on her face.

I looked at Olivia, "What's up?"

"That was Silvia," she said cautiously. "Mr. Camarena wants to see us in his office."

Carle looked at Olivia and then at me. She stood up, grabbing her purse. "Let's go see what Alphonso has to say."

We arrived to see him chatting on the phone. He motioned for us to sit down.

"Thanks, Jeffrey. I just wanted to get confirmation from you," Alphonso replied, placing the phone down.

For a few minutes he just stared at the phone, deep in thought. "Well, that is the craziest thing I have ever heard," he commented looking at them.

"*Porque, jefe*?" Olivia says.

"I just spoke with the lead counsel for the Sheriff's Department who confirmed that the parents and the Lakewood School District have agreed to settle," Alphonso said. "However, there are some pretty interesting requirements in order for it to be final."

"What are those?" Carle blurted out.

"It is quite the list," Alphonso said. "So, let me take them one by one."

Looking down at his scribbled notes, he begins,

"One, all parties agree not to discuss any matter of this case in the future under the government secrecy act.

"Two, all parties agree to sign appropriate non-disclosure agreements of an infinite lifetime.

"Three, all parties agree to shred nonessential forms and reports as agreed upon by the U.S. Department of Justice Attorney General.

"Four, all parties agree to maintain files related to all information in secured storage, accessible only through agreement with the U.S. Department of Justice Attorney General."

Alphonso looked up from his notes, "Finally, assuming all parties follow and abide by this Federal judicial order, monetary awards will be granted, and all legal bills paid in full."

We all stared at Alphonso. l am clueless as to the language spoken, but it didn't sound good. Carle and Olivia slowly get the picture that something big had just transpired.

Olivia spoke first. "Sir, why is the Attorney General of the United States now a part of this litigation?" she questioned. "And, how is this case related to anything pertinent with national security?"

l listened but didn't understand. "What?" I stammered. "How did this case become a national security issue?"

Alphonso stood up, buttoning his Ralph Lauren suit, "I think it's time that Saul and I go have lunch in town," he said walking out the door.

We stood up, uncertain what to do. Alphonso looked over his shoulder. "Don't do anything, and I mean anything, until I come back."

It had been almost two hours and Alphonso and Saul hadn't come back. We were all anxious and unable to focus on our work.

"Okay, you two get out of here. I can't focus on my other cases with you moping around here and looking at your watches every five minutes," Olivia commanded. "I will call you as soon as I hear from them."

l stood up, "Carle, you wanna go get some lunch?"

"Nope, I gotta burn some energy," shouted Carle heading out the door. "Surfs up!"

It would be another two hours before Olivia saw Alphonso walk into his office. Not wanting to seem anxious, Olivia waited patiently. Her phone buzzed.

"Yes, Silvia," Olivia looked down the hallway. "Okay, I'll be right down." Olivia closed out her computer and locked her file cabinet. She figured this would probably be a short conversation, and she was ready to go home.

Walking into Alphonso's office, Olivia could see the worry on his face.

"Olivia, welcome. Come in," he stammered. "Please close the door."

Sitting down, Olivia braced for the news. She knew inside that something big had happened, but she didn't know what.

"First of all, thanks for staying late. I assume you let Nigel and Carle leave early," he said.

"Yes, they were driving me crazy with all their fidgeting," she replied.

"Well, I wish I had more news, but I don't," Alphonso commented.

"Saul and I had lunch at Langer's hoping to catch some of the local gossip from law enforcement or the Feds," Alphonso sighed.

"We had a great lunch, but no luck in this case," Alphonso said, shrugging his shoulders. "Finally, we went straight to the Federal courthouse and tracked down the defense counsel for the city of Los Angeles. They had been brought into the case due to a jurisdictional matter and had taken lead on handling background litigation pertaining to the Los Angeles Sheriff's office."

Alphonso ran his hands through his hair. The silver showing a little more than usual Olivia noticed.

"We were told that our request for information on the Carnegie Mellon software got flagged by the Defense Technical Information Agency, who then informed a special unit linked with the Pentagon."

Alphonso continued, "An injunction was filed on behalf of the U.S. Defense Department by the U.S. Attorney General to cease all legal motions on this case in the name of national security."

Olivia looked at him perplexed, "A special unit of the United States Department of Defense got involved with this case?" she said. "Why?"

"Well, that is the million-dollar question, but as of this moment it is none of our business," Alphonso surrendered. "The parents and the high school were contacted directly by an official of some government agency who stated that while the merits of their case were valid, due to government secrecy laws, it would be best to have it dropped."

"With the caveat of some rather large monetary compensation," Alphonso added.

CHAPTER 24

Camarena, Chavez, and Rosenberg Office
Los Angeles, California
August 6, 1993

Several months later, we still hadn't gotten our heads around 'the why and the how' the Lakewood case got settled when Carle burst into the office. Full of rage and anger, throwing stuff around the office and slamming his palms against the desk, he seemed out of control.

I looked up from the newspaper, not quite knowing how to temper my friend, "What's up, brother?"

"Don't fuckin' call me, 'brother.' I ain't your brother," Carle snarled.

"Whoa, simmer down, Carle," I calmly spoke, not wanting to agitate Carle anymore. I kind of knew what was wrong.

I had been reading the article in the Friday morning edition of the Los Angeles Times about the civil rights trial for the police officers from the day before. Only two of the four police officers were found guilty for some strange reason.

"The two officers that were convicted will be fined $250,000, and they were sentenced to prison for violating Rodney King's civil rights," I said handing the newspaper over to Carle. "And, they might try and re-file charges against the other two some-time later."

Carle snatched the paper, not wanting to read it, but to throw it across the room. "That is a bullshit sentence, and you know it. They only got 30 months when Federal sentencing guidelines require at least 72 months at a minimum. Every one of those mother-fucking cops should be in prison for life," Carle said. "If they had been Black, they would have been hanged on the spot."

Carle hung his head down, his body trembling, resolved to keep fighting, "I just don't get it. With all that video footage and the other evidence, how could they not be found guilty of criminal assault?" Carle lamented.

l wanted to say something, anything, to help my friend. But there were no answers. Carle was correct. The Black man was fucked and had been fucked by this country for centuries.

Carle stood and headed over to the filing cabinet. He started digging through the drawers, pulling out files and toss-ing them on the desk. Finally, he found the file of most interest and waved it in front of me.

"Here. We can use this to help nail those motherfuckers!" Carle said heading out of the room. "It's about time we bring this information to light."

l got a quick glimpse of the file and realized the information Carle was talking about, "Carle, whoa, slow down. We can't share that. Remember?" l hurried after Carle. "We all signed articles of non-disclosure regarding that case."

"I don't fucking care. I need to do something, and if going to jail is the answer, so be it." Carle pulled away from me head-ing out the door.

The boss stood and walked around his desk, still shaken by the intrusion into his office and the conversation that followed.

"I'm sorry Carle, but there's no way the firm and interested parties can violate that non-disclosure agreement," he said. "The Department of Justice is not going to allow that to happen."

Carle looked at the boss, shaking his head in disbelief. The one man who he thought would understand didn't get it.

"Bullshit!" Carle spit out. "That is just bullshit. We must do something. We need to let the people know that we have the technology that can help identify the police officers in the video."

"Carle, I can appreciate your anger and rage, but there is just no way I'm going to let you get yourself and this firm into trouble." Alphonso moved Carle towards the door.

"Why don't you take a few days off, get a handle on yourself and your responsibilities as a servant to the legal profession." The boss gave Carle that 100-Watt smile, firmly closing the door between them.

Carle turned and walked towards the hallway. He saw the boss' secretary on the phone, looking at him with some concern.

"Okay, yes sir. I will see to that right away," the secretary spoke into the phone.

As Carle walked back to chat with Nigel, he heard Silvia say, "Security, we have a situation up on the sixth floor."

CHAPTER 25

Camarena, Chavez, and Rosenberg Office
Los Angeles, California
August 12, 1993

"What are you going to do now?" l asked Carle outside the office building. Carle had been gone for about a week and had just come back from human resources.

"I'm probably going to grab something to eat," Carle remarked.

"No, I mean, what is your plan for work?" l said.

"I don't know what I'm going to do," Carle said. "But they are going to give me severance pay."

"Why don't you go back and tell them that it was just a bad day, and it won't happen again," I pleaded.

"No, it is wrong that we can't share the information from the Lakewood and Los Angeles Sheriff's Department case. I can't ignore that any longer," Carle said.

"You go back inside and get with Olivia, she'll need all your attention now," Carle said, nudging me towards the office. "I'll call you soon and tell you what's going on."

l stood there, uncertain of what to do.

"Go," Carle said shoving me towards the door.

"Thanks, thanks for everything," l laughed.

Two weeks later Carle signed the final documents releasing him from his contract with the law firm. He got a decent severance bonus and a nice letter of recommendation.

One year later, Carle read the article in the Los Angeles Times with some satisfaction knowing that the original sentencing for the police officers convicted of violating Rodney King's civil rights was inadequate. It made him feel a little better about the justice system knowing that the 9th Circuit of the Federal Court of Appeals had vacated the 30-month sentence for the officers.

Sensing that the public needed some closure on the case, the U.S. Attorney General put together a defense team of impeccable standing, hoping to over-rule the lenient sentence handed down by the original sentencing judge. It would take some time to wind its way through the upper echelons of the judicial system, but Carle was confident that justice would be served.

To this day he still couldn't believe that the jurors could not recognize the police officers from the video taken during the night of the beating. As one legal expert later said, "It was ocular proof that the officers were at the scene, but eventually the jurors remarked that they just couldn't trust their eyes."

But then again, in hindsight, he realized that perhaps he was blinded by the anger of the situation, given that he knew the limitations of the face recognition technology. He and Nigel had seen it for themselves when they were given a demonstration by the Sheriff's defense counsel in 1993.

At the urging of the liaison with the sheriff's department, they had brought in photographs of themselves. The photos were scanned into the system and ran through the database matching process. Interestingly, Carle's photograph appeared to generate a higher number of positive hits compared to Nigel. The technician made a comment about the system having difficulties with grey-scale management.

"What do you mean 'grey scale'?" Carle asked the technician.

"Umm, the images for the database were taken from students attending universities involved with the project," the technician said, somewhat uncomfortable.

"And?" commanded Carle.

"Well, they are mostly Caucasian," the technician said stepping away from Carle. "Which means the database doesn't contain images of people with darker skin tones."

"You mean to tell me there aren't any Black people in your fucking database?" Carle yelled.

The technician looked at me. I just shrugged my shoulders, not wanting to get involved in this argument.

"Well, that is one of the main reasons why we're testing the system in Los Angeles," the tech said. "Given the diverse population of the community, the goal is to see if the system can learn over time how to interpret image tone and color."

"No, what you mean to say is that you want to learn how to control all the Black people by watching them," Carle said storming out of the demonstration room.

CHAPTER 26

Manhattan Beach, California
Spring, 1996

By 1996, Carle had worked for several law firms within Los Angeles and Orange Counties. He could just never quite find the right place or the right fit. After a couple of months, his contract would not be renewed, or the head of his department said they were downsizing. But he knew there was more to it. In fact, at one firm the human resources manager said that he was a little too militant for their firm.

Sitting in the booth at Uncle Bill's Pancake House just down the street from his condo in Manhattan Beach, Carle read the law review article about the recent Supreme Court decision related to the Rodney King case. The premise was that the original 1994 judgment against the two police officers was too lenient. It irritated him to no end reading the closing comment from the Supreme Court justices, "The short sentence given by Judge Davies was within the district courts discretion."

There was something wrong going on here. It seemed that no matter how many times the legal profession tried to make it right, something got in the way. And, it wasn't just the Rodney King case, he had seen it many times over the last three years since he left Camarena, Chavez, and Rosenburg.

Carle had represented hundreds of people of color arrested out of the Rampart Division of the Los Angeles Police Department. Many of the charges stemmed from the anti-gang unit, who seemed to take a strong interest in Blacks. There was talk of corruption within the force but never proven. All Carle knew was that in every case, the sentencing judges ruled in favor of the department and not his clients, regardless of merit or evidence to the contrary.

Carle looked down at his standard yellow legal pad. He had sketched out some items that needed clarification before he could proceed with his plan—a plan that revolved around the Lakewood case, a case that still pained him to this day.

Looking down at the pad, he reviewed the items again.

- What is the legality of the nondisclosure agreement?
- Look into the Government Secrets Act
- Find other examples of inherent bias reported for biometric assessment

Through visits to the Los Angeles County Library and extensive use of the legal documents and case law books at Southwestern School of Law, Carle was able to piece together the basics of the relevant court motions regarding privacy law, government secrets, and due process. However, he was not having much luck on the biometric angle. It seemed that most of the data on the mathematics and computer coding was locked up through other nondisclosure agreements or through patent law.

The only way he could get to the more sensitive data was to get the media to help him pressure the federal government to release some of the information. By late 1996, Carle felt that he had enough information to feel comfortable approaching local

Los Angeles television stations. They had been accused of ignoring local race relations over the past decade and were in
dire need for some good public relations. Not surprisingly,
most of them said no, but the consumer reporter for KABC
expressed some interest.

Carle felt exhilarated that he was finally going to make progress. He arranged to meet the KABC reporter at the Farmer's
Market off Fairfax and Third near West Hollywood. Sitting
down in preparation for the reporter to show up, Carle was
anxious. Was he really going to be able to shed light on the
issues related to people of color in Los Angeles? Would the
Lakewood case regarding face recognition technology be of
interest?

Carle sat on his surfboard enjoying the sun and the motion of the
sea. He loved the smell of the ocean and sounds of the seagulls
flying overhead. He realized now that he had wasted too much
time on issues of which he had little control. The loss of a good
job, good friends, and money made it all a little more bitter.

Luckily on this day, Carle was no longer considered an outsider floating off Manhattan Beach. He had been accepted by
the local 'boarders.' They shared the waves with the him, just
another brother riding the energy of the sea, day in and day
out. In fact, thanks to Carle, there were many other boarders
of color that had emerged on the shores, not that they were
given any less grief.

Hearing the waves slap at his board and feeling the surge ride
underneath, Carle thought about his life after leaving Camarena.

It had been almost four years, and it hadn't gone quite as planned, but it wasn't too bad. He was getting more surf time, which was a positive.

He was having problems finding a firm that would hire him on a full-time status, so he did mostly contract work, here and there. It paid the bills, and he was sure thankful that he bought his condo years ago, but he wasn't quite making a difference like he promised Grandpa Harper. Besides, the whole thing with Rodney King and his termination from the law firm still bothered him, not to mention that the local news agencies had no interest in the Lakewood story about face recognition.

He reflected on that day at the Farmer's Market when he was going to divulge the information to the KABC reporter. He was so nervous and anxious about the meeting, but in the end, it lasted only 10 minutes.

"I'm sorry Mr. Harper," the Black reporter said. "But we just don't find the story compelling enough to run with it."

"Why not?" Carle asked in disbelief.

"It's just not relevant anymore," the reporter said standing up to leave. "And, Carle, in your own best interest, I suggest you just forget about it."

Scanning the shoreline, Carle got to thinking about the first time he saw this beach. He had just moved out from Atlanta and had found an apartment instead of moving in with his cousin Wayne. The first morning he walked down to the beach and saw the boarders hanging together off the shore. It seemed like such a cool thing to do.

"Yo, bro, welcome back," said one of the local boarders bringing him back to reality.

"Thanks, good to be back," said Carle.

"Dude, you still at TRW?" the boarder asked.

The question made Carle think about how long it had been since he had been on his board.

"Nah, man. I haven't been there in about 5 years," he said.

"Right on. Seems like yesterday, bro," said the boarder as he caught the next surge.

Carle thought about that. Yes, it did seem like yesterday, but so much had changed.

Looking back to check the next set, Carle got to thinking about his time at TRW. It was the perfect time and the perfect place for Carle. It gave him security and eventually the chance to pursue his legal career.

Feeling the ocean surge, Carle began to paddle to pick up speed to catch the approaching wave. Stepping up on his board to catch the swell, the solution became abundantly clear.

He needed to learn a little more about The Falcon and the Snowman.

Carle reflected on that day in Manhattan Beach when the idea popped into his head. He had been floating on his board, soaking up the sun, when that dude asked if he still worked at TRW.

It was such a random question, a question that eventually landed him as a guest at Lompoc. He last worked at TRW about five years ago, so to hear that name brought back all those memories of working there. One of the fondest was the story of the Falcon and the Snowman about a couple of guys who decided to make their country pay for all the bull shit it had been spreading around the world for decades.

It was then and there that Carle realized that their story was the answer to his problem regarding the Lakewood and Rodney King connection. Since the local and national media had no interest, perhaps getting the Russians involved might get their attention.

Of course, when the Lakewood case was settled under the auspices of government secrecy, they all had no idea what was going on. Alphonso did not know and didn't care. Olivia was just as dumbfounded, but she had other cases to work on, so it didn't really matter. Nigel had decided to move on, so that left it up to Carle.

Carle was desperate to get something going, so he was willing to try anything to get the Russians interested. He was sure they wouldn't give a fuck about some Black dude getting beat up, but they might find some value in the mathematics behind topological surface assessment. Wasn't that what Nigel said formed the basis for facial recognition technology?

It was a long shot, but Carle had thought about this issue for far too long to just walk away. Sadly, it was a plan that would eventually get the attention of the FBI and of little interest by the Russians.

It had taken a couple of months to get up the courage and work out the details of the pitch, but Carle stood outside the Russian embassy in San Francisco.

He learned from doing some research at the Los Angeles County Library that the Russians had spent quite a significant amount of time and money on the Pacific Coast region in the

17th and 18th centuries, stretching from Alaska down to San Francisco. But competition with the British firm, Hudson Bay, and the continued uprisings by the Native Alaskan tribes forced Emperor Alexander II to relinquish all control of his Russian American colony.

The land sale started first with Fort Ross near San Francisco in 1842 and ended with the final sale of Alaska to the United States as negotiated by the Secretary of State William H. Seward. Carle found it fascinating as he had never learned much about California's rich history while growing up in Atlanta, Georgia.

The Russian government would not have a major diplomatic presence in San Francisco until the early 1930's after financial difficulties made it necessary to close the consulate in 1924. It wasn't until 1934 that the Soviet Union purchased a new building in San Francisco. The consulate would be in the posh neighborhood of Pacific Heights, not far from Fisherman's Wharf and the Presidio. This location would eventually serve the Soviet Union and its allies during and after the Cold War. A valuable location indeed, not only because of the wealth and affluence of the neighbors, but because of its height overlooking much of San Francisco.

In the movie, *The Falcon and the Snowman*, they made it seem that Boyce and Lee just walked up to the Russian Embassy in Mexico and started sharing secrets. It took several months just to get noticed and many more to start a meaningful dialogue. Part of the problem was that the Russians just couldn't see how two young college students would have anything of value. Eventually, Boyce was able to sneak out some very classified information that got Moscow's attention.

Carle didn't have access to anything like what Boyce and Lee were able to deliver, but he had a story and some details of the computer simulation software that he found on some computer bulletin board. It was the best he could do with limited time and money. Besides, he didn't really want to develop a relationship with the Russians, just use them.

Pushing through that front door of the Russian Embassy in the fall of 1996, it became quite clear that there was one little detail of the story that he neglected to consider. Standing in the main foyer with people all around, there was one thing that he could not hide—that he was a Black man.

PART TEN

CHAPTER 27

Silver Spring, Maryland
September 11, 2002

The General paced back and forth. It had been a year since their death, and the thought of them stranded on top of the North Trade Tower haunted his dreams.

Dorene had called him that day as they walked up towards the rooftop. It was the standard protocol for the World Trade Towers should any fire emergency occur between floors 70 and 90. Dorene had gone to visit her sister, Eileen, who worked at one of the investment firms in the North Tower.

Well, it was Dorene and their daughter, Margaret. They were going to have lunch at the Windows on the World restaurant to celebrate Margaret's 12th birthday.

It was something that Margaret had wanted to do ever since Eileen got the job at the firm.

The words still crept into his mind at night...

"Daddy, I'm scared. People are saying we're going to die."

With tears in his eyes, all the General could say was...

"It's okay, honey. Mommy will take care of you. The firemen will come get you soon."

Before he could speak with Dorene again, the cell signal

dropped out. Later he would determine that it was about the time the tower started to collapse.

Like the tens of thousands of surviving family members, the General was numb for months. The loss of Dorene and Margaret was one thing, but to think of how they perished was enough to push any man or woman over the edge.

It was hard to believe that the perpetrators had lived and trained in this country. In fact, some were even known to be on the federal watch list but tracking and surveillance were difficult. In addition, the practice of verifying photographs inside passports had not been determined as viable. Or, at least that is what the media had been told.

For the past 10 years he had spent millions of U.S. taxpayer dollars and man hours watching former U.S. service members so that there would never be another Oklahoma City. Come to find out, they were looking in the wrong places and watching the wrong people.

When he read the New York Times article last month making the case that the Bush administration had been given warning about the possibility for the World Trade Tower bombings, the General had to contain himself from screaming. The words of Margaret fueling his anger.

"Daddy, I'm scared. People are saying we're going to die."

It was that day when the General realized that ever since West Point, he had been working for the wrong ideals and the wrong people. These people weren't interested in him, or Dorene, or Margaret. No, they were just interested in their oil, their real estate, and their wealth.

Staring out the window of his office onto Colesville Road, the General decided it was time to do the right thing. The elitist establishment had been governing within the Beltway for too long without reprisal. They needed a wakeup call. And, looking down at the request form in his hand from California, he was reminded of a surveillance project that he had forgotten about from long ago. A project that had been funded by the Department of Justice, using software from Carnegie Mellon University.

The purpose was to use face recognition technology to help identify undocumented immigrants in Los Angeles in support of the Immigration and Control Act. It was a project that had received very little interest within the intelligence community in Washington, DC until the Los Angeles Sheriff's Department agreed to use the technology for a criminal case related to male high school students in Lakewood, California.

What partially made the General take notice of such a request was the origination: Lompoc Federal Penitentiary.

Sitting in his Maryland office, the General reread the transcript requested by an inmate from this penitentiary. It was for information about a project conducted by the Drug Enforcement Agency in Miami, Florida in 1999. In all his years he had never heard of this project while running the counter-intelligence operations program in the domestic affairs section at the Department of Defense. This position afforded him unlimited powers and a budget to rival any domestic and foreign intelligence program in the world.

The mission statement for this counter-intelligence unit said it all:

"To maintain the integrity and respect of the United States military establishment, the counterintelligence operations program will…

"...make sure that the skills and expertise derived from military training and service will not be used against the United States government and citizens therein.

"...monitor the activities of military members through surveillance of domestic partnership programs such as the Veterans of Foreign Wars, Disabled Veterans of America, the Veterans Administration, and any groups held in association with military membership.

"...manage and coordinate all information with local, state, and Federal programs related to domestic and foreign terrorism."

To help monitor and track service members, the General and his group had investigated almost every viable option within the scientific community. So, it was hard to believe that the DEA project existed without his knowledge. The General read the summary one more time.

"The face recognition software developed out of the University of Illinois proved reliable in matching digital composite drawings with the photographs held within the database. The software program had a success rate of 93% with an error variance of 2.87% for all photographs within the database. When separated by ethnicity, the success rate for identification was highest for Caucasian images (98%) and lowest for African American images (48%). Images for Hispanic and Asian images scored within the variance of the program, providing accuracy of 70%.

"In further testing, the face recognition software was deployed at the Miami International Airport August 30, 1999 with testing completed by August 30, 2000. The project's main priority was to determine the feasibility and accuracy for identifying known members of South American drug cartels from face images within the INTERPOL database.

"During the 12-month test period, there were 13,345,839 individual images collected at the Miami International terminals. This represented 98% of the known ticketed passengers arriving or departing from the airport. Of these, 567,259 images were flagged as potential candidates with further screening reducing the potential candidate image pool down to 43,590. The final assessment with known drug cartel personnel images held within the INTERPOL database revealed a 100% positive match for the 2337 individuals traveling on fraudulent passports.

"In summary, the use of the face recognition program proved reliable and accurate with a 7.7% margin of error when compared against standard mug shots or face images collected from surveillance cameras within the airport. While these tests are preliminary, it is highly recommended that this software system be implemented throughout the United States at all primary entry points for foreign travelers whether through air, train, or sea."

The General thought about the implications of the transcript. It appeared that the Drug Enforcement Agency and the University of Illinois had developed a face recognition system that would have identified that the 911 terrorists did not match the information contained inside their passports. They would have been stopped from entering the airport and they wouldn't have been able to fly those airplanes into the Twin Towers. Dorene and Margaret didn't have to die.

Sitting in his office in Maryland that day in 2002, he decided it was time to take a trip out to California, to the coastal town of Lompoc and the Federal Penitentiary. Picking up his phone, "Mary, can you get me a flight out to Los Angeles as soon as possible?"

CHAPTER 28

Carle walked through the back entry of the visitor center without expectations. Nigel had been the only person from his past that has made any contact with him including his family. In fact, they disowned him altogether when they learned that he allegedly sold American secrets to the Russians.

Stepping into the hall near the back entry, Carle stopped and submitted to the search. It had become common for inmates to smuggle stuff out of prison as much as prison officials found people smuggling things into prison. So, the inmates must submit to a search entering and leaving the visitor center.

Carle walked to Window 14 and sat down, wondering who would actually come visit him in late summer. Carle felt the bead of sweat roll down his forehead. Wiping his face with his bare arm, he could feel the heat and humidity. The late summer heat along the California coast could get quite warm, and Lompoc wasn't known for its air conditioning.

Nigel visited just a couple of months ago, so it couldn't possibly be him. Nigel had become his touchpoint to the world, sending a steady stream of letters and packages containing books and articles. It proved immensely helpful for Carle's sanity.

He was hoping it wasn't another reporter wanting to get a quote about Christopher Boyce. It seemed like every time there was a news report about espionage, someone would dredge up the story about the Falcon and the Snowman, which ultimately led them to Lompoc and the request to meet with Carle.

Boyce had escaped from Lompoc almost 16 years ago, so it wasn't like they could compare notes about selling secrets to the Russians. Besides, after being captured in 1981 in Port Angeles, Washington, Boyce had been sent to Leavenworth to serve out his time. His stay in Leavenworth was short-lived due to several beatings, forcing Boyce to experience numerous stints within the various Federal prisons. Little did Carle know that on this very day, Christopher Boyce would be released from the correctional facility in Oregon after serving his 25-year sentence.

Carle was startled from his thoughts when the chair across the window made a sound.

"Hello, Mr. Harper," said a distinguished looking older gentleman in a nice dark suit.

Carle slowly opened his eyes, thinking he was having a dream. Before him sat an older man with the look of military or law enforcement. Not good.

"Hello," grunted Carle.

The older gentlemen looked around the visitor room. The rows of cubicles stretched out across each wall.

"Mr. Harper, it appears you have been looking into some pretty sensitive files pertaining to face recognition surveillance. Again!" the old man said.

"Yeah, so what? It is all within the Freedom of Information Act of 1974," Carle provided. "It ain't illegal."

"Well, given your conviction for selling secrets to the Russians and your prior issues with a non-disclosure act relating to a legal case down in Los Angeles, you aren't doing yourself any favors," the older man said looking around.

"And, why the fuck should I care what you think?" Carle yelled, seeing the visitors and inmates look his way.

"Everything okay in here gentlemen?" a young prison guard queried through the door window.

"Yes, it's cool, Jerry," Carle said.

"Because, Carle. I might just be the one guy that can get you out of this shit hole," the older man said.

"Bullshit," Carle said. "I've heard that before."

"No, really. Listen to me," the old guy said pulling his chair closer to the window.

"Go on," Carle said, "I got all day."

"I had a chance to look into your sentencing case, and I think there are a couple of ways we can get the courts to overturn your conviction or at least get you out early," the old guy said.

"How so?" Carle asked.

"There is no mention in any of the filings that you actually transmitted any government secrets to the Russians. Furthermore, the courts did not accept the evidence provided by the lead DOJ counsel regarding the disclosure of fiber optic locations."

Carle listened to the old guy for about 10 minutes. "Yes, all that stuff is in my appeals summary," Carle said. "What do you have that is new?"

"Well, the fact that their lead witness was compromised and, in fact, has been charged with espionage himself," the old guy offered.

"Dimitri?" Carle said.

"Yes, it appears that Dimitri was involved in several illegal activities, besides serving as station director for the San Francisco Russian Embassy."

"Interesting. What else you got?" Carle asked.

"I think we might be able to get some leniency related to the Lakewood case," the old guy said. "I have found information that might be helpful regarding the validity of the case being classified as a government secret."

Carle shook his head. He had heard this story before. Just tell us what we want to know, and you can get out of here. "What's the catch?" he asked the man.

"Well, the catch is, I get you out of here, and you work with me showing that the U.S. government could have stopped the World Trade Tower terrorist attack by using the University of Illinois technology," the older man said. "And, along the way we get that bull-shit espionage conviction thrown out."

"Okay, times up gentlemen," said the guard. "Carle, you got about five minutes to finish up, and then I need you to step out into the hallway–palms up, legs spread."

At least this guy could see that the espionage case was a sham. That was one thing in his favor. Carle stood up. Looking directly at the man. "What's your name?"

"You can call me General," Old Guy provided.

"Well, General. You get me a little more information on how you think I can get out of here early, and we might have a deal." With that, Carle turned and walked out of the booth.

But, before the door closed, he heard the General say, "Give me some time, but I will come back, rest assured."

CHAPTER 29

Lompoc Federal Penitentiary
Lompoc, California
December, 2002

It took longer than planned, but when the old guy came back a couple of months later, he outlined an idea of how they could get Carle's sentence reduced for time served.

Carle listened, engaged more as legal counsel than as the defendant. If what this 'General' guy says was true, then there was no way that the appeals court could deny their motion.

The General placed a couple of pictures down on the table. Carle didn't know how the old guy arranged it, but they were able to use the private room within the visitation center. Looking around it seemed more like a boom-boom room for conjugal visits, but it did offer them privacy.

"Any of these guys look familiar?" the General asked.

Carle looked down at the pictures. Immediately, Dimitri stood out from the crowd.

"Yes, that's Dimitri!" Carle said, pointing to Dimitri.

Dimitri Bezrukov was the first guy that Carle met when he was finally taken into an office when he walked into the Russian embassy long ago.

"Good. Just checking," he grunted. "Anyone else?"

Carle looked down at the other five photographs. They were a bit fuzzy and grainy, but he could make out the faces.

"This guy looks familiar. I think he hung around the embassy quite a bit," Carle said.

"Bingo," said the General. "Meet Detective Gerrard Kopcheck of the San Francisco Police Department and the local liaison with the DEA and FBI."

"It seems these two fellas had quite the racket going on in San Francisco. Evidently, they run Russian prostitutes out of the major hotels in town and provide cocaine to help get the party started," the General said. "Dimitri brings the girls in under diplomatic immunity, supposedly to work at the Embassy, but then turns them into junkies where they turn tricks all day and night," he continued shaking his head.

"Gerrard, God Bless his soul, takes care of the hotels by extorting them with trumped up health and safety violations. And, then gets them to donate free rooms for the girls," the General said. "And, I got a lead that says they are in cahoots with a DEA agent for the free drugs. We got a bunch of douche bags right here."

Carle looked down at the photographs shaking his head. "Well, that is quite the story, but how does it relate to me?"

"Well, Dimitri and Gerrard are what we call 'social climbers,'" the General said. "They are always looking for ways to look good in the eyes of their superiors."

"Yeah, so what?" was all that Carle could say.

"Well, on the day you showed up at the Russian embassy, they were in a bit of a bind and needed a little diversion. Unfortunately, you were in the wrong place at the wrong time," the General said solemnly.

The process to submit a request for an early release through the Department of Justice took almost nine months. At times Carle just wanted to give up, but the General and many of his fellow inmates kept pushing him forward.

It was instrumental that Carle had a legal background, but it still required hours and hours of research looking at case law related to evidence presented with matters related to national security. Luckily for Carle, when he reached out to Dr. Hopkins, his old mentor at Southwestern College of Law, he got not only Hopkins but the help of several faculty members as well.

Actually, Carle never did provide any information to Dimitri. After their first meeting at the Russian Embassy in late 1996, they had a few meetings at various hotels throughout San Francisco. It became clear that Carle really didn't have any technical knowledge of the software system, which irritated Dimitri immensely.

"What do you mean, you not know code structure of operating system?" Dimitri asked one night.

"Hey, I told you early on that I am not a computer guy. I just have access to the computer code that is being used for topological surface evaluation," Carle said, impressed with his use of 'topological.'

"What can you tell me about fiber optic traffic around Silicon Valley?" Dimitri asked. "Can your system detect patterns of underground fiber cables?"

Carle paused for a moment, trying to think of something to say.

"Yeah, it can do that," he lied. "Our system can pick out shading differences related to where people stand, it can surely pick up some differences related to cable systems."

"Yes, you say that, but I don't believe you," Dimitri said. "You looking for more money?"

"No, I don't care about the money," Carle said. "I mean I like money, but what I really want to do is show the world what the United States is doing with this technology to the people of color."

"I don't care about people of color," Dimitri said. "I want to know about fiber cables. But if you help me, then I help you. Okay?"

"Yes, I understand," Carle said reluctantly.

"Okay, I set up another meeting next month with guy who can help," Dimitri said. "Try to bring some information to show him you are serious."

Carle shook his head. "Yes, I can do that. When and where?"

"I will let you know," Dimitri said standing up from the table. "You want Russian girl for night?"

"Uh, no," Carle said. "I've got an early flight back to Los Angeles in the morning. But thanks anyways."

"No problem," Dimitri said. "My gift to you. Next time, maybe two girls."

"Yeah, sounds fun," Carle said heading towards the door.

Dimitri watched Carle walk away, smiling to himself. He did not think Mr. Harper could deliver, but he had another idea that was perhaps even more valuable.

Carle caught a cab outside the hotel and headed towards his hotel by the airport. It would be a long night and a short flight. He would need to think about what he could bring to the next meeting. It had to be something believable.

Unbeknownst to Carle, the number one priority of the local FBI in early 1997 was preventing the Russian government from finding those underground fiber optic cables. Besides classified government data traffic, the expanding world wide web was increasingly using the fiber optic hubs that were based in and around San Francisco. Why bother tapping into a cable under about 5 miles of ocean, when you could set up shop in cozy Pleasanton or Sunnyvale using a simple plug and play adapter?

It would be a major coup if the Russians could tap into them or worse, destroy them.

Carle looked around at the books on the shelves and the plaques on the walls of the Lompoc warden's office. He had been allowed to come here every now and then and get a few books on case law. There were a few times when he came to help others, but most of the time he came to help himself. The warden read from the judicial order,

"Carle, I am instructed to release you from your sentence on this day, July 1, 2003. You have served four years of your five-year sentencing. Your early release reflects your good behavior and serving the needs of your fellow inmates. In addition, the court accepts your request for early release as part of an arrangement with the U.S. government."

"Thank you, sir," Carle said looking forward, a learned response in a place where just a quick glance could get you killed.

Warden Peppers looked up from the document,

"Carle, on a personal note, I want to commend you for serving your sentence without malice or disruption. You have been a bright spot in an evil place. And, I want to thank you for all of the incarcerated souls that you helped during your time here at the Lompoc."

Carle looked at him. Not quite knowing what to think or do. Warden Peppers came around his desk, arm out-stretched with an open palm, "Carle, congratulations. Let's get you out of this shit hole."

The warden escorted Carle down the hall and out towards the main entrance, but in this case, his exit to freedom. He guided Carle down the passageway stopping just short of the last doorway before saying, "And, Carle, go out and do something good."

The Blonde Lady waited patiently while Mr. Harper worked his way over to the car. This was her first assignment with the General, and she needed it to go smoothly. It had taken her two years to arrange for this gig, and she wasn't going to let the opportunity be wasted.

When the General told her that she needed to pick up Mr. Harper at the Lompoc Federal Penitentiary, she didn't know if he was serious. But a quick search on the Internet provided all the information she needed.

The Lompoc Federal Penitentiary near Lompoc, California is considered a low-risk facility. The surrounding area is located on a coastal peninsula of central California, just west of Solvang and the Santa Ynez Valley. In fact, besides fruit orchards and the burgeoning wine industry, Lompoc itself isn't well known.

On the other hand, mention Vandenburg to anyone in Southern California and they will immediately light up. Vandenburg Air Force Base is known for launching most of the department of defense satellites, often offering Southern California residents spectacular colors in the late evening sky. In fact, Vanderburg had been deemed the West Coast launch and recovery base for the Space Shuttle in the early 1980's, until it was determined that the local earthquake fault line proved problematic.

As a low-risk facility, it offered inmates an easier life with training and rehabilitation. Carle Harper was one of these inmates.

Carle looked at the black limousine waiting at the prison gate. He slowly approached the car, unsure about the situation but thankful that someone was here to pick him up. His family had pretty much disowned him once he was officially sentenced.

"General says hello. I will drive you to hotel," said the Blonde Lady. "My name is Chanel."

"Uh, huh," grunted Carle, not used to a person being so cheerful and not carrying a gun.

"Right this way," Chanel said, reaching to grab his paper satchel. Reflexively, Carle pulled away.

"Okay, you hang on to bag," she smiled. "Let's get out of heat."

She opened the door allowing Carle to slide inside. She was doing the chauffeur look, and doing it well, thought Carle. As Carle closed the door, he saw Warden Peppers looking at him. Thinking about the warden's last comment while closing the car door, Carle laughed to himself. Do something good, he mused.

Chanel stepped on the gas, and they were off. He looked around. Hanging on the right passenger door was a suit, shirt, and tie. On the floorboard, a box with some new black shoes. And, right there in the middle, his final request: An In-N-Out Double, Double, smothered in onions, a side of fries, and a chocolate shake.

CHAPTER 30

Hyatt Regency Hotel
Westlake Village, California
July 2, 2003

The limousine pulled up to the hotel. It had been a quick trip down from Lompoc. They must've been going pretty fast, because Carle didn't remember driving through Santa Barbara.

Chanel threw the car into park and exited the driver door. She came around the car and opened his door. "Welcome to Hyatt, Mr. Harper," she said. "General has booked room for you."

She reached in and pulled out a small suitcase that Carle had not seen. "Please follow me to check in," she commanded. "Pick up clothes, don't worry about mess from Out and In. I clean for you."

Chanel strutted over to the reception counter.

"Mr. Harper has reservation under name of General McCallum," she said, pulling out some documentation. "He has room for three nights."

The Front Desk Dude looked at Carle and then at the blonde trying to figure the situation out. Satisfied, he looked down at his monitor. "Yep, right here it is," he beamed. "Fifth floor, king-size bed."

Looking at Carle, Front Desk Dude said, "Breakfast starts at 7 AM tomorrow, and tonight the dining room is open until 9 PM. But if you want something to eat, I suggest getting over there around 8:30."

"Everything is covered for three days," Chanel said looking at Carle. "The General will come here tomorrow around breakfast time. He will meet you in lobby. 8 AM sharp."

With that, Chanel turned on her black stiletto heels and walked out towards the limo. Her legs made Carle remember how much he enjoyed the female form. Carle leaned down to pick up his suitcase.

"That is one hot looking limo driver, buddy," Front Desk Dude whistled. "You're one lucky guy."

"Uh huh," Carle grunted as he headed towards the elevators. "That's me alright, one lucky guy."

Stepping off the elevator on his floor, Carle did realize that he was one lucky guy. His time in prison was looking bleak before the General showed up. And, he was still amazed at how the old guy was able to gather some of the information that they presented to the United States Attorney General.

All Carle had to say was that the old guy kept his word, although his intuition was telling him something different. Pushing the door to his hotel room open and flipping on the lights, he was reminded of what his mom used to say to him when he was in trouble, *'Son, you done jumped out of the frying pan and into the fire.'*

"Good morning, Carle, happy fourth of July!" the General said. "Don't you look great! Nothing like a good night's sleep."

Carle just stared at the General, not accustomed to the friendly behavior so early in the morning.

"Well, let's get some breakfast," the General said, standing up. "I'm starved."

Carle looked around, still trying to process that he was out of the Lompoc. He, in fact, had not slept all that great. It was sound or lack thereof that was the problem! It is what those in prison found most absent when they first get out.

Not because it was soothing, but because sound fore-warned danger. The danger of an approaching inmate, coming to claim your life or your virginity. Both of which Carle had to endure during his time in prison.

"Carle, are you going to get some breakfast?" the General said with concern.

"Uh, yeah. I was just taking it all in. Being out of the Lompoc takes some getting used to!"

"I understand completely," the General said. "Take your time."

I doubt if you do, Carle thought.

"Sweetheart, can you get this man some coffee and orange juice?" the General took control understanding that in prison decisions were made for you. Choice was not an option.

Carle and the General sat silently while they finished their breakfast. The General noticed how Carle placed his fork in front of his plate and the saucer covering the coffee mug. There was a ritual to it, but he couldn't figure it out.

"Why do you have your fork in front of your plate?" the General asked.

Carle looked down, "To show that I'm not hiding it," Carle replied. "In prison, it helps those around you feel comfortable seeing your fork on the table."

The General shook his head in confirmation, "And, what about the coffee mug?"

Carle laughed looking at the coffee mug, "Oh, that's just an old habit from law school," he said removing the saucer. "It just helps keep the coffee hot!"

The General burst out in a deep laugh, "Hah!"

Carle looked at the man sitting across the table. He didn't really know much about him, and their conversations over the past several months had been more directed at his release. There was something about him that made Carle feel uncomfortable, but he couldn't put his finger on it.

"You must be good at digging stuff up," the General reflected. "Is that how you found the information about the DEA Miami project?"

"Yeah, I'm pretty good with a computer," Carle said. "But the DEA thing was a fluke."

"What do you mean by a fluke?" the General asked.

"Well, I was searching through some case files to help one of the guys when I was at Lompoc to help appeal his case. I had typed drug deaths in Miami, but it did an autocorrect to dea Miami," Carle said. "I got this really long list of cases that made no sense to me. But, halfway through the second page was mention of a DEA project in Miami using face recognition for identifying cartel members."

"You gotta be shitting me," croaked the General.

"Nope, it's true," Carle said. "I took it as a sign that I was meant to see it."

"Is that when you ordered a copy of it through the defense archival system?" asked the General.

"Yeah, I made the request a couple of weeks later. I was afraid

I was being set up, and then I just figured what does it matter? I'm already in prison," Carle acknowledged.

Carle and the General sat at the table looking at each other for several minutes. Breaking the silence, the waitress came over with a coffee carafe. "You fellas want more coffee?" she asked.

"Yes, ma'am," they said at the same time.

"Jinx," the waitress said.

"Pardon?" Carle said.

"When two people say something at the same time, you say Jinx!" the General replied with a faraway look.

"It's a game my daughter and I used to play a long time ago," he offered.

"You have kids?" Carle asked. "Did. Margaret," replied the General.

"But she and my wife died in the World Trade Tower attack."

"I'm so sorry to hear that," Carle replied.

"Thank you. It has been a long, lonely struggle," the General sighed.

"Why are you so interested in the Miami DEA case?" asked Carle.

"Isn't it obvious?" the General said with a tear in his eye. "If that damn system had been in place, those terrorists wouldn't have made it onto the planes. And, they sure as hell wouldn't have flown those planes into those buildings."

"Yea, I agree that there was a cluster somewhere regarding the implementation of the Miami face recognition system," said Carle, "but we can't assume that it would have prevented the towers coming down."

"No, don't say that," the General cried out. "Margaret and Dorene would still be alive!"

People sitting around them looked over cautiously. Not quite sure what to do.

Carle waved and gave them a big smile. Then, he gave a thumbs up sign. Most of them smiled and went back to their food, but one older lady gave him a very dirty look. *Fuck you, bitch*, thought Carle.

"I'm sorry," Carle said. "I really feel sorry for your loss. I just remember reading that the Miami project did not get much notice inside the beltway in Washington, D.C. It just seemed that they wanted it to fail."

"Exactly, that is why we need to uncover the truth, Carle," the General said. "Because those sons of bitches have been doing that for decades."

Carle looked at the General who was looking a bit crazed, making him feel a little uncomfortable.

"That is not going to be very easy," Carle said.

"I have faith in you, Carle," the General said. "Besides, we have something else in common."

Carle looked at him. "And, what is that?"

"The distrust of our government, knowing that they have been complicit in protecting the interest of the establishment, the elites, and themselves, instead of the people," the General said.

"You are correct. I do not trust our government, but I don't care about the establishment or the elites," Carle said.

"I think you will when you know the truth, " the General shared. "You see, the same technology that could have been used to save Margaret, was the same technology that could have convicted those police officers in the Rodney King criminal case."

Carle stared at the General. He couldn't believe what he just heard. "How the hell do you know that?" Carle asked.

"Because I'm the one who had the Lakewood case classified as a national security threat," the General answered.

Carle couldn't believe this was happening. It was hard to comprehend. "You mother fucker," Carle said grabbing the knife off the table and standing up. "I spent 4 years in prison because of you."

"No, Carle. You are the reason why you spent 4 years in prison," the General said. "And, as we just proved, it was the FBI and the Department of Justice that helped seal the deal. So, sit down and listen to me."

"How can I believe you?" Carle said sitting back down.

"Son, you're just gonna have to trust me," the General said. "I didn't know you were a part of the Lakewood case until your request for the DEA project came across my desk. I wondered why you had an interest, so I looked up your sentencing case and did a little digging."

"Why haven't you mentioned it over the past ten months?" Carle said.

"Because I didn't want to muddy the water. I felt that if I shared that with you too soon, you wouldn't trust me."

Carle's outburst had gotten some attention from the other guests and the serving staff. "Everything okay here?" said the Front Desk Dude from yesterday.

"Everything is fine," the General said. "My friend here just learned some news that was upsetting to him. But everything is good now. Right, Carle?"

Seething inside and confused, all he could say was, "Yeah, we're all good."

PART ELEVEN

CHAPTER 31

I waited around the foyer of the Face Value building for an hour or so before heading up to the fifth floor. I am not wearing a face covering, but I see that many of my co-workers are still following the CDC guidelines including social distancing and hand-sanitizer ad nauseum.

I took the elevator up to the 5th floor. Company policy only allowed four passengers per trip, but I was by myself, so it didn't really matter. Stepping out of the elevator, I whistled inside my head. The small lobby, just off the elevator, is impressive with Persian rugs hanging on the walls and a nice mix of French and 9th century Moroccan furniture.

It appeared the Professor didn't require the need for a receptionist, as there was no one in the lobby area, just several nice upholstered chairs and a sofa in a dark green fabric. I felt out of place knocking on the immense wooden door, wondering if I could even be heard.

"Come in, come in," l heard from the other side of the door. Slowly pushing open the heavy door, I walked into the next room, wondering what to expect of my next journey.

"Welcome, Mr. Grant," I heard a voice from deep within the room. "Come over here and sit down."

Peering deeper into the room, l could faintly see a figure of a man standing before an exceptionally large desk.

Professor Gallegos comes around the desk to meet his new authenticator. "I see you approve of my collection," he said sans face mask.

"I am so pleased to meet you. Bernadette has spoken so highly of you," the Professor said, "and, there aren't too many candidates that achieve authenticator III at the onset. So well done, chap!"

"Uh, thank you. It's an honor to meet you, sir," l responded, falling back on decades of strict military bearing when meeting superiors.

"Sir, my ass," snorted the Professor. "Call me Doc like everyone else."

"Sit, sit." Doc glided me around the room and down onto a chair.

"Okay, sir," l responded.

"Doc, and that is an order," he said. "Now enough about me, let me hear more of your story."

For the next 40 minutes or so, l described my life from being born in Oklahoma to moving every three to four years with my family around the United States to my undergraduate study at Cal State Northridge.

"And, what year did you start your MBA at Boston University?" asked Doc.

"2000," I replied. "I had worked for a law firm in Los Angeles, and I realized that the legal field just wasn't of interest."

Doc looked down at his desk, "Well, I see about a four-year gap between the law firm and the start of your MBA. What did you do?"

"Well, I did close to three years in the Peace Corps down in Peru, where I helped set up a water irrigation system up in the mountains," I said. "Then taught for one year at a community college while I prepared for the GMAT exam."

"That must have been pretty dangerous," commented the Professor.

"The community college?" l questioned.

"No, no. Your time in Peru. Wasn't the Shining Path starting to make themselves known in the region?"

"Yes, sir, err, Doc," I said, correcting myself.

"They often came around to our field camps, but they were most appreciative of our work and pretty much left us alone. However, this was before they started to use more violent means of getting themselves known." I reflected on those times, remembering how lucky I was that last month.

"Nigel," he said.

"Sorry, I was just thinking about a most unpleasant time towards the end of my assignment," l whispered.

"Can't wait to hear about that later," said Doc, "but we have lots to cover, and I need to get out of here by 3 PM. I promised my wife that I would take her out to dinner at a reasonable hour for a change."

"Yes, happy wife, happy life," I remarked. Not that I ever had that luxury.

"Exactly, and we try to live that motto here at Face Value," Doc affirmed.

"Now, let's see. You aced our photo recovery test," he said.

"Only about 5% of our candidates do that. So, you are in a small minority. I believe that qualifies you as a *super recognizer*!"

There is that term again that Greta mentioned to me. "Excuse me, what is a 'super recognizer'?" I asked.

Doc turned around and looked at me. "It means you have an innate ability to detect facial features and identify them out of context at an accuracy rate better than any face recognition algorithm currently in practice around the world," Doc shared. "It's the extreme opposite of those suffering from prosopagnosia."

"Prosopagnosia?" I questioned.

"Yes, that is the scientific name. The more common term is face blindness," said Doc. "People lacking the ability to recognize people, even family members. A quite common trait to tell you the truth! I think 1 in 50."

"Oh, okay," I said. "That is not me. I am fairly good at remembering my family and just about anyone else."

"I'm sure, and that's why it's a pleasure to have you on the team," Doc acknowledged. "Plus, your prior work with Black Matte Technologies."

Oh, crap, I thought. Here we go again. He could see the look on my face from the question.

"Bernadette tells me you are pretty sensitive about this topic, and I understand given any nondisclosure documents you might have signed," the Professor said candidly. "However, just know that we handle many top-secret accounts and will respect the boundaries of your agreements."

"Okay, I understand," I said. "I have had some personal issues with people not abiding by their non-disclosure agreement."

"I assume you are talking about your friend Mr. Harper?" Doc queried.

"Yes, how do you know about Carle?" I asked.

"I think Bernadette told you we do a pretty thorough background check on our candidates. And, that often includes prior work history and colleagues." Doc replied.

"Yes, she did mention that to me," I said.

"Well, let's move on from that topic," he said. "Nigel, why do we need to even worry about face recognition?"

The question made me pause for a moment. During the entire interview process, I had never asked that question.

"Well, I do know that it has great value in helping law enforcement identify criminals. And, I suspect it must be helpful screening large numbers of people like in airports," I said. "But, in general, I don't think there is any real value of face recognition for society."

"Good answer. It does have extreme value for law enforcement and crowd control. But it's use for general purposes is often questioned," Doc said. "Most people believe it encroaches on their constitutional rights for freedom of expression, which actually isn't one of our rights."

"Yes, I do know from prior experience that the issue of personal privacy when it comes to anything related to one's image is controversial, going all the way back to the late 1800s," I said. "With the use of social media websites, people often fail to realize that they are giving away ownership or their privacy."

"Well said. It is amazing what people post of themselves on Facebook or Instagram," Doc said.

"Now let me show you a little bit of our surveillance program and how you as an authenticator fits in," Doc said, standing up and walking over to a humongous monitor while talking,

"In a general sense, face recognition stemmed from more of

an exercise in image detection. Scientists have been interested in understanding how the human brain detects and recognizes faces. And, with the advent of computer processing, it was just a matter of time before some kind of external machine would be used.

"I won't bore you with all the details, but you can imagine capturing and interpreting how the brain processes data was very limited until the advent of micro-electrodes and computer processing. It was only natural that we would use these tools to help us collect data. Always to help understand the brain and human development.

"For example, how does a baby detect an image? Research shows that developmentally they focus on basic features of an image–size, shape, color. Then as the brain begins to form more connections between the different sensory organs within the central nervous system, they soon learn to associate more complex relationships of image like distance and structure. An example might be looking down on the earth. At first you would notice the color of the ocean and land, but eventually you would start to notice the contour of the landscape.

"And, how does an image then become a face? The view of the eyes and nose, possibly the ears, is replaced by the distance between the eyes and the shape of the nose in relationship to the contour of the face. Naturally, it is more complex than that, but you get the idea. And, from a face to a person, it takes the connection of all the senses plus a little context. Think 'loving mother, angry father' concept. The baby might only experience warmth and affection from the mother, so a pleasant experience develops. Whereas for the father, they usually assist sporadically and uncomfortably, more than likely offering expressions of discomfort or anger.

"There is a lot of information processing going on, which the human brain can handle but proved limiting for early machine learning experiments. Now, fast forward to the mid-1990s and the rapid increase in computing power, and machine learning, or 'artificial intelligence,' allowed for incredible advances in the understanding of face recognition.

"The ability to detect an image using the various three-, four-, or six-point markers became simple and fast. This was instrumental in the early development of digital cameras, if you pushed the action button slightly, you could center the picture through the reflectance of the eyes."

"Oh, yeah. I remember those days. I had totally forgotten about it," I said. "I was terrible at it. Half the time I would just click through and take the picture. You kind of had to have some skill to be able to use that feature, if I remember."

"Exactly, the early versions of the digital camera were clunky and often had issues with the detection system. Most people thought that the main feature of those cameras was storing the image digitally. While useful, it was only a fraction of the technology that was incorporated into those cameras," Doc provided.

"Not to mention millions and millions of unnecessary pictures, in my opinion," I shared.

"True. I always imagine the future when aliens come down and find all these flash drives, hard drives, and servers with billions of data bytes of goofy pictures. I can only imagine them wondering why it took so long to colonize earth," Doc said, taking a sip of his coffee.

"That's funny," I said. "Along with an equal number of doggie poo bags in land-fills."

Doc just about choked on his coffee laughing, "Oh, that is so true."

"I can see you and I are going to have a good time, Nigel," Doc said. "While I get us some coffee, think about what emotions you can identify when you look at a person's face."

"Wow, that would be great," I said. "I could use some coffee about now."

"Great, are you a bold kind of guy or more a medium blend?"

"I like more of a medium blend," I said.

"Okay, cream or sugar?"

"Uh, nope, just black, please," thinking what a twist to have the CEO get me coffee.

I sat down near his humongous desk and watched him walk over to a counter in the corner. It looked like he had one of those higher-end Nespresso machines, but I wasn't sure. All I knew was that the coffee was going to be good.

Handing me a standard corporate 'Face Value' mug, he said, "Well, what emotions do you see?"

Honestly, I hadn't really had much time to think of his question because I was looking at the awesome view from his window, "Well, I haven't really categorized all the emotions I have seen, but I would imagine most people can recognize sadness, fear, anger, and elation.

"Bingo," he said. "Pretty much the four main visual cues that were documented decades ago. Now do you think any of those can give you the intent of the individual expressing them?"

Hearing that question made me sit up in my chair. I hadn't really ever thought about intent before when looking at people, but I suppose people do that as part of a survival instinct.

"The only one of those that makes me think I could predict their behavior would be 'anger,' I said. "The other three seem more passive in nature, but anger always seems to lead to action."

"Damn, Nigel. You continue to make Bernadette look brilliant with your hiring."

"Well, she did screen me pretty thoroughly," I admitted. "Actually, at times it felt like an interrogation."

Doc laughed. "She has been known to make a few people cry."

"Now, suppose you were a country, and you were worried about having your citizens defect. How could you prevent that from happening, but still allow them to move about freely?" he queried.

"I suppose you would just watch them!" I said.

"Yeah but think of the cost of that task. Is it one observer to one person, or one observer to 10 people?" Doc said.

"Uh, that's a good question," I admitted.

"Well, take a look at this short summary report from INTERPOL and see what the Chinese government did during the 2008 Beijing Olympics," he said, handing me a folder. "I need to go to the bathroom."

Executive Summary
INTERPOL Committee on Face Recognition Technology

Date: November 21, 2008
Topic: Face Recognition Control in Beijing
Author: Erik Van Orden, Ph.D. and Simon Gallegos, Ph.D.
Staff: Yin Qi, Ph.D.

BACKGROUND:

The Chinese government was challenged with maintaining order and control of their Olympic athletes during the 2008 Beijing Games. The government was making great strides on the world stage in terms of economic growth and prosperity. But their efforts internally would be jeopardized should there be a sizeable number of athletes trying to defect during the 2008 games.

A Japanese company, NipponFace, was brought into partner with the government-controlled company, WFU Technology. NipponFace boasted that their system had a 90 percent success rate for detecting individuals within a crowd and modest success identifying people who exhibited suspicious behavior. The Chinese government had also requested that the WFU system match images collected during the games with photographs taken of the athletes participating in the games. The Chinese government deployed the WFU Technology throughout the Olympic athlete village and the individual sport venues.

AFTER ACTION ASSESSMENT:

The information collected from the WFU Technology during the Olympic games was kept confidential from the International Olympic Committee and participating countries. The WFU system collected an enormous number of digital images throughout the games. The WFU/NipponFace machine-learning algorithm was able to detect and digitize over 85% of the captured images as individual faces. These individual faces were then stored at a data center arranged by the Chinese government.

In an internal report prepared by NippnFace and shared with the face recognition community, it was reported that the NipponFace system was able to detect over 95% of images as faces. Further analysis revealed that 3% of captured faces identified individuals exhibiting suspect behavior. However, there was no information as to the types of behaviors.

Additional information was obtained through various intelligence networks within the Chinese government and supporting agencies from various national governments. This information was obtained through verbal communication from individuals with access to the system files or confidential documents.

There is some disagreement as to the accuracy of the NipponFace system with estimates ranging from 23% to 78%. The limits of the NipponFace face recognition system were attributed to several factors: the inherent bias related to grey tones, feminine features, and surprisingly, face coverings. Evidently, there was an influenza outbreak at the beginning of the games, so visitors and the athletes started wearing face masks. This caused a high degree of false positives throughout the games, although it was not reported in any summary material.

CONCLUSION:

The scope and size of the challenge provided by the 2008 Beijing Olympics showed the promise for face recognition, regardless of the reported accuracy. It is felt that the Chinese government will continue to develop and deploy this system throughout China to help control and curb dissent.

"What do you think?" Doc asked.

"The coffee is great. Just the right amount of flavor," I responded.

"No, about the summary document from the 2008 Beijing Olympics," Doc asked.

"Oh, yes. It's quite interesting," I said. "I seem to remember hearing something about identification problems but nothing as troubling as this report suggests."

"Indeed," said Doc nodding his head in agreement.

Doc and I finished off our coffees and chit-chatted a little about San Diego.

"I actually grew up in El Cajon, just east of here," he confided in me.

"Oh, is that a big deal around here?" I questioned.

"Well, in some circles yes," he chuckled. "El Cajon was always the step-child of San Diego proper, the in-between place between the gold coast and the gold in the mountains out further East in Julian."

"Whether east or west, you still had to go through El Cajon," he said with pride. "Actually, there was a lot of farming and ranching throughout most of its history, but like many towns in Southern California, El Cajon really bloomed after World War II."

"Ah, location, location, location," I said.

"Yes, El Cajon offered people a chance for cheap land and maybe a dozen or so citrus trees," Doc said, seemingly in a trance.

I imagined he was playing back his time in El Cajon. "Ha," he said, startling me. "I showed them."

"How so?" I questioned.

"Well, nobody took me seriously when I started acing my math exams in high school, not even my parents," he said.

"But my science teacher at El Cajon High School believed in me and introduced me to a mathematics and computer science professor at UC San Diego," Doc reflected. "Professor Schmidt was well-known around the world for his understanding of linear algebra as it applied to fluid dynamics."

"That does sound pretty impressive," I acknowledged.

"Indeed, it was. Without Smitty, I wouldn't have gotten a full scholarship to CalTech," he laughed.

"I am a firm believer that at some point in every successful person's life, there is one person who helped them get to that next level," I confided, still looking forward to that day.

"Nigel, I agree," he said. "Now let's talk about how we can put your natural gift for identifying faces to good use."

CHAPTER 32

Face Value Headquarters
San Diego, California
January 11, 2021

Doc and I walked over to that beautiful wooden desk. "I really like this desk," I commented. "The wood grain is so incredible. Where did you find it?"

"You like it?" Doc said. "I know a guy up in Bishop who has access to federally protected land. He is the only one that can go in and clear out trees that have fallen. Part of a fire mitigation process."

"Oh, that is cool," I said.

"Yes, indeed," Doc said. "It's amazing how old some of those Scrub Spruce and California Oaks are."

Sitting on top of the wood countertop were two of the largest computer monitors I had ever seen in my life.

"Wow," I said. "Those are huge."

"Yeah, I don't splurge that much, but I do like big monitors," he replied. "Plus, it helps with the eye strain."

"I would imagine," I said.

"Nigel, why do you think people are so much better at picking out faces in a crowd than what a computer can do looking at an image or a video?"

"Uh, I have no idea," I answered.

"Context," Doc said.

"Context?" I questioned.

Doc said, "Let me explain,

"I will start with the easy part. An image from a camera or a smartphone is stored as a series of picture elements or pixels. Each of these pixels represents an image value depending upon the intensity of light and the refraction of the wavelength within the light. This gets stored pretty much as a one-dimensional array.

"An image seen through the lens of the eye is still a collection of pixels related to wavelength and intensity. While it stores the image within the visual cortex of the brain, this image block is also connected with all the other sensory information from that same time stamp. So, an image of a rose is stored along with the smell of the rose, the color of the rose, and the temperature of the environment, and so on.

"There is one other element that separates a human from that machine. And, that is the emotion of the environment from which it was taken. Some liken it to the electricity in the room and others have suggested the pheromone-like connection, but it is this feature that helps people determine whether a person is happy or sad. Angry or afraid.

"So, what makes you and all the other super recognizers better than all those fancy algorithms is context. While you might consciously notice that the nose or chin or eyes have a pattern, what you subconsciously process is everything else associated with the picture."

I stood there trying to take this all in. I had never ever thought about how I remember things.

Doc asked, "When you are in a room full of people, how do you remember their faces?"

"I don't know. I guess I take a mental picture of what I see all around and then try to place the person in the picture by what they are wearing, what they are doing, what they might be saying," I confessed, "I don't really know, though."

"Exactly," Doc offered. "We really don't know how your kind remember faces, but we do think it has to do with the context or the environment that is presented to your memory centers."

Not comfortable being lumped in with *your kind,* but I guess he did have a point.

"Okay, I understand. Usually when I remember a face or a person, I just don't think of their face," I said, "but I place them in the setting—the supermarket, the bookstore, the coffee shop."

"Bingo," Doc says. "That's what separates you from a machine and why you are so invaluable to us, especially now given that the use of face coverings due to the coronavirus is so common."

"How?" I asked.

"A video camera installed at an airport or a mall or anywhere will just store a one-dimensional replication of the light transmitted from the image, the amount of light reflected and absorbed. The image has to be presented to the camera at just the right angle or the system won't be able to detect the standard five-point pattern of eyes, nose, chin, and mouth," Doc said. "If that can't be done, then the image is blurry or unrecognizable."

"Okay, that makes sense. Photography 101," I stated.

"There are two fundamentally important elements that give the human brain an advantage in such a situation," Doc said. "Hear me out,"

"First, from the day we are born, our brains are learning patterns from sensory cues: smells, sounds, touch, and sight. This builds our neural network that forms the basis for our cortical connections. Our brain is controlled or driven by the organ that sends it the most data, which happens to be visual information.

"This can be considered an early development progression related to survival. If you could see and make out that a dinosaur or sabre tooth tiger was heading your way, you lived. If the pattern was fuzzy and unidentifiable, well, your gene pool did not move forward.

"During the development process, one of the emotional constructs of human behavior is personal attachment and intimacy, resulting in a lot of face viewing. So, at an early age we detect and associate the simple three-point pattern, eyes and nose, in the context of the state. Warm and comforting, for example. The process continues where we add the mouth and then the ears to further refine and define the identification of friend or foe.

"When we talk about machine-learning, especially in regard to face recognition, scientists from around the world have been trying to replicate this process so that machines can figure out how to learn in decades what humans have learned over millennia."

"Holy shit," I said sitting down. "Sorry."

"No problem," Doc said. "It is quite fascinating when you get down to the physiology of it all."

"Let me get this straight," I said. "People in general are far better at picking out faces because they have been using some kind of innate identification process related to survival."

"Yes, that's a good basic assumption," Doc said.

"So, do us *super recognizers* have a wiring difference in our visual learning center that makes it easier for us to store or recall the image?" I offered. "I'm a little fuzzy on that part."

"Spot on," said Doc. "We aren't quite certain about the differences, but recent MRI brain images and PET scans of people trying to recognize images suggest that there is a larger neural network within the hippocampus of those considered 'super-recognizers.'"

"Hippo-what?" I asked.

"Hippocampus," Doc said. "It's a small area in the dead center of the brain that helps connect all the sensory input—touch, movement, hearing, temperature, vision."

"Uh, huh," I responded.

"Interestingly, there is some even newer data which suggests that the amygdala is twice as large in super-regs than normal people," Doc said.

"What is an amygdala?" I asked.

"It's a small part in the central region that controls and regulates emotion, mostly fear and aggression," Doc said.

"Okay, you've mentioned emotion before. What's the connection?" I asked.

"Well, it is unknown, but some believe that this enlarged amygdala allows for more information to be processed along with the image," Doc lectured. "It kind of boosts the image storage or perhaps even adds a third dimension to the data point."

"That would make sense. It would seem to validate your prior observation that people, or us super regs, seem to have an edge due to emotional cues," I said, feeling quite brilliant.

"Well done, Nigel," Doc said, "and, at the present, that is something we can't build into a machine."

"You mentioned two elements that us super-regs had. What's the second one?" I asked.

Now I could see why Bernadette took a liking to me, she knew I had a big amygdala.

"The second element that super-regs have, heck, people in general, is storage capacity," Doc provided.

"Storage capacity?" I questioned.

"Let me explain," Doc said.

"Since time immemorial, people have always been fascinated with understanding how we store information in the brain. From rats to dolphins to people, the brain is the most curious and amazing organ. This is evident when you get to dissect a sheep brain in anatomy and physiology. The structure of the brain itself and the delicate nature of the tissues don't correspond to something that has about 100 terabytes of memory storage."

I had to stop him right there. "Pardon me, did you say 100 terabytes?" I asked.

"Yes, it's all conjecture, but a conservative estimate is 100 terabytes, although current thinking from PET scans suggest it might go up to 1 petabyte in some people," Doc replied.

I looked around, not remembering what a terabyte was. Seeing my discomfort and uncertainty, Doc provided, "One terabyte is equal to 1000 gigabytes, and one petabyte equals 1000 terabytes."

"Wow," I said.

"Exactly, over the past few years having 1 terabyte storage in a computer has become economically feasible for most people. But, peta-size storage is a different animal altogether," Doc answered. "Think about most computer rooms or data centers, what do you see?"

Again, my mind was blank.

"Refrigeration. They need massive amounts of cooling to keep the servers from melting," Doc said. "For the most part, our brain can store tremendous amounts of data without worrying about the issue of overheating."

"Okay, so there's a storage issue, but how does that relate to face recognition?" I asked.

"Let me continue," Doc said.

"We mentioned that the camera images don't have as much information processed along with the image itself like we find with mammalian images. But, even so, there is still a tremendous amount of information.

"You might remember the early days of television and those old black and white TVs. To get good reception, you normally had to tweak the antennae to get the signal and then adjust the raster to improve the resolution of the image on the glass screen.

"The raster is just the electron beam painting the image or intensity from a copy of the image onto the screen, activating the phosphorous coating on the inside of the glass.

"Now, fast forward to today. There isn't too much difference about how an image is determined between raster technology and digital format. In both cases, light waves that are detected cause some change. Instead of activating green phosphorus to show the image on a monitor, digital images turn the intensity of that light beam into a numbered coordinate on a matrix. Kind of like in your algebra class where you had to graph two points 1-0 and 0-1.

"With digital imagery, what you end up with is a giant matrix from the picture elements that represent the image. A normal matrix of 720 by 360, for instance, has about 259,000 pixels or 0.3 megapixels. Now, scale that up in size to improve resolution, and we are talking terapixels.

"And, it is those pixels that need to be stored with each image. One might say that the technological development of digital photography far exceeded our ability to store and access information on a hard-drive.

"Today most storage is solid-state storage, or s3, which uses electrons for storage, allowing for speed. But, even s3 cannot handle the size of high-resolution images."

"Sorry for going so deep into the technology, but I find it helps my super-regs understand and appreciate how they fit into the system," Doc offered.

"No, it's fascinating. I never took a computer class in college, so it's all new to me," I offered. "I've heard of some of the terms, but never how they're all connected together."

"Great to hear," Doc said.

"Let me see if I get the gist of what you're saying," I said,

"We store more information pertaining to an image or memory than a standard digital camera. People have larger storage capacity than current technology today. And, I assume we can access that image faster than what is feasible today, even with s3 technology."

"Spot on again, Nigel," Doc said. "And, don't forget that people, and super-regs in particular, can access an image better and faster than a machine."

"Ok, now I get it," I said summarizing my thought,

"People, or super-regs, can look at a crowd and pick out a face faster and better than having a camera take an image of that crowd and then match it in some database. A person can have a more in-depth understanding of the context of the crowd than what can be interpolated by a machine.

"I would assume that people have a higher success rate and less of an error rate when trying to identify a specific image within a larger image."

"Well done, Nigel," Doc said.

"Thanks for the confidence," I said. "But, I'm a little fuzzy on how machines or algorithms have been so successful in the past. Aren't they already at maximum in terms of understanding?"

"You are correct that face recognition software has been quite successful and robust in terms of identifying images from social media posts. The turning point for being able to use stored digital files for image assessment came about in 1988 when two mathematicians applied a technique, they had developed for identifying bubble patterns with fluid dynamics to large data matrices," Doc said.

"I won't bore you with the mathematics, but basically they converted the digital points into linear vectors, which reduced the amount of data for storage. This reduction was huge in terms of being able to store and then retrieve images for comparison."

"I get it. Kind of like a zip file," I said, impressed with my analogy.

"Sort of. A zip file takes out data that is redundant and converts that to a common variable. Then all you need to do is assign a value of the stored data along with the common variable. It squeezes it down. Kind of like dehydrated food. You take out the water and get powder. When you add the water back, you get a close proximity to the food."

"Ah, okay. But, when you rehydrate powdered milk, it doesn't look or taste like fresh milk," I said from experience.

"You are absolutely correct," Doc said. "In the early years, it took a while for the mathematics to get that common variable exactly right, so when it came time to reconstitute the image, the resolution was not as good. But, now the math behind the equations has been improved."

"Well, that's good," I said.

"But, as discussed, we need to figure out how to put 'context' into the equation," he summarized.

"Nigel, I've got to head to a meeting, but I'm very impressed with your quick assessment and understanding of the material," Doc said. "Let's meet tomorrow and go a little deeper into what challenges lie ahead with face coverings becoming more accepted in public spaces and how an authenticator like yourself fits into the equation."

"Okay, sounds like a plan," I said. I turned to head out of his office, but had one question, "What is the name of the mathematics, so I can do a little homework?" I asked.

"Eigen assessment, which consists of the eigenvector and that common variable, the eigenvalue."

I stood at the door, watching the words come out of his mouth, but not quite hearing what he said after he said *eigen assessment*. Oh, brother, here we go again!

CHAPTER 33

When Doc said 'eigen assessment' yesterday I felt the hairs on the back of my neck stand up. I hadn't thought about that word in a very long time.

I remember spending a lot of time that first year at the Camarena law firm working on the Lakewood case, most of the time looking at individual rights concerning ownership of self. I had tapped into my gap year in the United Kingdom and my experience looking at 17th and 18th century portraiture.

Looking at classical paintings of the Victorian age and the busts from the Egyptian and Greek periods made me realize how people have always valued the human form. Oddly, the works of the famous Italian renaissance artists consisted more of the female form than the male. Botticelli, Titian, and Raphael were consumed with representing women as angels or mothers. On the other hand, men are depicted as warriors or slaves.

One might say that the most recognized face in the world is that of Jesus, perhaps with Mona Lisa a close second. A great number of famous painters have attempted to paint their view of Jesus and his disciples. Jesus is most always painted as a man even though there are some that suggest that Jesus was a woman. Where is the proof besides pictures that Jesus couldn't have been a woman? There are no first-person accounts of verifiable substance that can be used unless one views the Bible as such a document.

In any case, the human connection with the 'face' is something that has stood the test of time. In fact, there is some evidence suggesting that the appreciation of 'human form' was first observed in northern Africa some 3 million years ago. More recently, works resembling visual likeness of face and form are attributed to the Upper Paleolithic Europeans some 125,000 years ago. However you think about it, people like looking at themselves.

I was heading up the elevator to Doc's spacious office. I was feeling surprisingly good about our last meeting and appreciated his perspective on the development of the face recognition process. Knocking on that gigantic door, I could hear his familiar response, "Come in, the door is always open."

"Welcome, Nigel," Doc said. "Good to see you again. Ready for some more background information?"

Doc met me with his firm handshake and a nice fresh cup of Nespresso.

"Yes, sir," I said, forgetting his request for informality. "I've had a chance to do a little homework on eigenface vectors and their use with face recognition."

"Excellent, can't wait to hear what you have learned," Doc said. "But first, I have a question."

"Shoot," I said.

"Well, Nigel," asked Doc. "What do you remember from the Lakewood case?"

I sat frozen in the big leather chair. I looked at my arms laying on the armrest, feeling the rich leather underneath.

"Nigel, cat got your tongue?" Doc asked.

"No, I just haven't thought much about that part of my life in a long time," I offered.

"I understand that," Doc said. "Let me be more specific, what do you remember about the face recognition system being tested by the Los Angeles Sheriff's Department for the Lakewood Police Department?"

Again, the non-disclosure agreement and Carle's time at Lompoc made me a little reticent about answering his questions.

"Nigel, it's okay," Doc said. "I get your concern about the agreement but understand that our company non-disclosure provides you protection."

"Well, okay," I said. "In that case, I guess we can talk in general terms, but I request the option to say, 'no comment' if I feel uncomfortable with your questions."

"Fair enough," Doc said.

I began to summarize,

"First, my understanding of the process and their system will be filtered by the information I have learned along the way and during my training here at Face Value.

"From our talk yesterday about the storage component necessary for face recognition programs, I can see how the system being tested by the Los Angeles Sheriff's Department must have been very rudimentary. The processing speed alone must have made it excruciatingly slow and cumbersome for the staff and technicians.

"I remember learning about the work of Woodrow Bledsoe from the 1960's, who in some circles is considered the father of face recognition. I think he proposed the use of 10 face identifiers as a standard template: The center of the pupils, inner and outer end points of the eye, nose, and chin."

"Yes, yes," said Doc. "Woody was a leader in the field. I had the pleasure of meeting him towards the end of his career. He had retired from the Panoramic Research Group to set up a private consulting business.

"Yes, I remember reading something about his time at Panoramic. It was all hush-hush with funding coming from an unnamed source," I said. "I think most people thought it was the CIA, while others thought it was the FBI."

"Or both," Doc said. "But imagine, Nigel. In those days they laid a photograph on a digitizing grid, and then using an electro-magnetic wand pressed down to mark the face identifiers. The digitizing grid then took those markings and converted them into geometric coordinates."

"It is mind boggling for sure," I replied and continued,

"During our early research on the face recognition software for the legal case, my friend Carle and I went down to the facility where they were working on the process. The technicians were helpful and told us how the number of identifiers went from the 10 suggested by Bledsoe to 21. The increase in face identifiers helped provide a better understanding of the face but with a much greater need for speed and storage.

"The one thing that sticks out today is when they compared my photograph in the system with that of Carle's. We couldn't understand why his photograph kept getting an error message with the system. The technician told us that when image coordinates of the new image could not overlay onto the coordinates of the stored image, the result is an error message. That is when he told us that they had problems with 'darker tones' and why they were testing it in Los Angeles.

"Carle and I couldn't really grasp it at the time, but now I know it's because of the shading bias problem with people of color in the face recognition databases. When Carle pushed a little more and the guy mentioned 'darker tones,' Carle went ballistic, shouting about controlling Black people."

"Yes, sadly much of the shading bias still exists today, along with more delicate features found with female images," Doc offered.

"Yep," I said. "I read a few research papers last night about light reflection and shading."

"A good example I like to use is that of looking down on the Earth from space," Doc lectured,

"This is long before astronauts were in space and could provide that 'contextual' observation of what the surface of Earth looked like. The Blue Pearl so to speak.

"While we were still trying to figure out how to get satellites into orbit and have them stay in position in a particular orbit, a group of enterprising geologists and meteorologists were devising a project to map the surface of the earth.

"These pioneers understood that a better understanding of the Earth's topography would be helpful for weather forecasting that would be important for transportation, agriculture, and military use. Besides the hurdles related to speed and storage, they had to develop an understanding of the various colors represented on the surface. In addition, problems were encountered when looking at areas with high elevations. It wasn't so much the high plateaus that caused problems, but that higher peaks casting shadows as the Sun traversed its path along the surface of the earth."

"Yes, I came across a few citations related to topography and face recognition," I said. "However, most of them said that topography doesn't require the amount of detail needed to accurately identify the fine detail normally seen with face identification."

"That is very true," Doc said. "And, now let's talk about your job as an authenticator."

"But first, more coffee," Doc said, walking over to the Nespresso machine.

"A day without coffee is like a day without sunshine," I said.

"No truer words were spoken," Doc agreed. Doc walked around the office, stretching from side to side and shaking his arms and legs.

"My God, if I don't move around, I can feel my body tighten," he said with legs apart bending over to touch his left foot and then moving over to the right.

"You start doing some of those yoga poses we talked about?" Doc said.

"Not yet, but I plan to get started soon," I said. I didn't really want to tell him I wasn't a yoga guy.

Doc finished and whispered, "*Namaste.*"

"Okay, where were we? Oh, yes," he said.

"Thankfully, we've gotten that shading problem worked out and have reduced our error rates by almost 90%. I am certain that in our system we have gotten rid of the error bias seen with feminine form.

"And, development of the 'contextual' component within our system is moving along, thanks to the input from our early authenticators. I think you will see this over the next few months as you begin to compare your experience with our face recognition system.

"That still leaves one unanswered question. Do you know what that is?"

"Umm, no," I said hoping not to disappoint.

Doc continued,

"Again, we've worked through most of the challenges with face recognition technology relating to the image, the storage, validation, and assessment. We still have problems when there is too much noise around an image in public settings. That's where the 'contextual' concept from super-regs come in.

"But now that the use of face coverings is becoming so common, we must change the metrics we use for detecting and matching. The use of face coverings removes the chin, mouth and jaw profile often found in most face recognition models. They accentuate the eyes and forehead but alter capturing the nose. Even ear profiles are contaminated due to elastic bands that are used to keep the face mask in place.

"You've got to imagine there's been a large sum of money invested into this technology from private foundations, corporations, governments and unnamed sources. At one point it seemed that the system was close to perfection, but the COVID-19 pandemic has really caught the intelligence community flat-footed.

"There have always been challenges with criminal organizations working on ways to defeat face recognition systems, from baseball caps, wigs, sunglasses, and even cosmetic surgery. But, given the acceptability of face coverings, the criminal element has risen to the occasion to take advantage of it.

"I'm on the biometric committee for INTERPOL, and at our last meeting it was determined that the threat from criminal activity has increased month over month since the outbreak in early 2020. They have used face coverings along with other measures to defeat our border security checkpoints and crowd control. No matter how many changes we've made to software technology, we are still losing the battle.

"The INTERPOL 2021 Project was convened for the express purpose of finding a way to improve our technology and along the way identify and apprehend individuals considered threats. With that charter, it was determined that we needed to enlist the services of individuals with uncommon aptitude for detecting and remembering faces.

"Luckily, Face Value had been moving towards hiring authenticators or 'super-recognizers' to help us understand the contextual side of face detection. So, we have been chosen by INTERPOL to take the lead in determining the feasibility and viability for using real-time assessment, along with standard face recognition systems for identifying criminals.

"And, that is where you come in, Nigel. You're the only authenticator we feel comfortable sending into the field at this time. We feel you can help us learn how to discriminate those who mean no harm, from those that do. And, you have an uncanny skill using contextual assessment for understanding the environment within a situation. You will seek out those faces that possess characteristics not consistent with our algorithms. Once you identify these people, we have a security team that does the rest."

I sat in the chair trying to process what I had just heard. "Umm, this sounds more like an active process than passive viewing," I said. "I don't know if I am quite up to the job."

"Nigel, you are perfect for this job," Doc replied. "And, there really isn't much danger in the process for you."

I sat perplexed by what I had just heard. Wondering if this was really the kind of thing I wanted to do. It seemed that there were a few things that Bernadette had left out during the interview process.

"What is the number, do you think," I asked, "of those not within the INTERPOL database?"

"Less than 5%," Doc offered. "A very manageable number."

"Yeah, that is a pretty small number," I said. "What does this security team do once a person gets identified?"

"Short story, they get photographed and released," Doc said.

"What's the long story?" I questioned.

"Best you do not know," Doc glared at me. "Nigel, you are helping everyday citizens be a little safer. You get to travel and enjoy a genuinely nice salary and benefits."

"How does my work make people safer?" I asked. "What are you not telling me about the 5%?"

"Well, we estimate that about 60% of the 5% are violent criminals," Doc offered. "So, their identification and capture can get a little dicey. But, once we get them off the streets, so to speak, it does make for a more safe and secure world.

I stood up. My head started to spin again. The information was a little overwhelming to me.

"I'm sorry, but I need to take a break and think about this," I said.

"No problem," Doc said. "But, Nigel, while you think it through, just consider this–your ability to detect and remember faces is our only hope to make the world safe."

"I see," I said. Walking towards the elevator to go down to my office, I was struck by two things.

One, his use of 'our only hope,' and two, I didn't know if I was up to being a superhero and a super-recognizer!

PART TWELVE

CHAPTER 34

Carle approached the meeting with the General with caution. He just didn't have a good feeling about what was going on. It had been almost three years since they last met, and Carle hadn't actually worked for him in about four years.

But then again, when the General wants to meet, there really isn't much Carle can do about it. Helping get Carle out of prison was just the first step towards digging his hooks deeper into his skin.

They met at the Westin Hotel on Century Blvd. It was a convenient location for both. The General was flying from the East coast for the meeting and then heading right back out. For Carle it was a breeze, just a hop over the Santa Monica mountains, from Northridge down Interstate 405, and he was there.

The General was waiting for Carle in the hotel lobby as planned. He still had the military bearing of a soldier and was dressed in an expensive looking suit.

"Welcome, Carle," the General said. "Good to see you again."

"Hello," Carle said with a little less enthusiasm.

"Let's go get some lunch. I'm starved," the General said. "The food served on that plane was pathetic."

Carle doubted very much that the General flew coach, so for him to turn down breakfast must've meant it was bad. "I'm pretty hungry myself," Carle replied.

The host sat them at a table away from the crowd at the request of the General. They looked at the menu slowly getting comfortable with each other. It was standard airport hotel food, simple, quick, and fattening.

"How's the knee holding up?" the General asked.

"It's feeling better, thank you," Carle said. "I had some meniscus damage from college football. I was having problems with my knee locking every now and then, so I just had them go in and clean it out."

"Damn football injuries," the General said. "The amount of money these schools make off these young players is outrageous. College sports just isn't the same anymore. It's all about the money."

"Yes, I agree with you," Carle said. "Hopefully, the new rule that the NCAA is considering will help make it right."

"What rule is that?" the General asked.

"They are working out the details, but the NCAA is looking at allowing individual athletes to get paid for the use of their name, image and likeness," Carle offered.

Well, I'll be damned," the General said. "I hadn't heard. It's about time these college kids get credit for their own image. It's a brand just like anything else. It will allow them to negotiate a deal at face value, instead of letting the schools take all of the proceeds."

The waiter came and got their order and refreshed their coffee. One thing they did have in common was their love for coffee. Carle had to chuckle seeing the General cover his coffee cup with his serving dish.

"Nothing like a good cuppa Joe," he said.

"Amen to that," Carle replied.

"Carle we are entering some interesting times," the General said leaning closer to Carle. "This impeachment process with President Trump is starting to gain traction. I hear reports from inside the Beltway that the impeachment trial will begin sometime later this month. There is a big push to dis-credit the President sometime late summer.

"Uh, huh," Carle said. "I don't really give a shit about the election."

"You should, Carle. If people thought the 2016 Presidential election divided the country, wait until they see the division generated by the upcoming election. Joe Biden can't seem to escape the damage from his son, Hunter. And, all the Democrats got is Warren and Sanders, two Democrats with some crazy ideas. That only gives the incumbent more leash to spew his filth and lies. Come November, there are going to be a lot of unhappy people when he wins again. Just think how much more polarized this country is going to get," the General said, perhaps a little too loud as people looked their way.

"I agree with you, sir," Carle said. "But what's this got to do with me?"

The General looked around and launched into his delivery,

"Well, for one, the impeachment is a smoke screen. It's just a way to keep attention away from something big. I don't know what exactly, but the China trade agreement isn't going over very well. And, the Democrats keep hammering the Trump administration and anyone that will listen about the Russians meddling in the 2016 election. No one seems to give a shit about that or that Putin is trying to extend his power base as President of Russia until 2024. In the intelligence world, many believe that Putin has some damaging information on Trump, allowing Russia to do just about anything they want without reprisal."

Carle nodded in agreement. "Yeah, I've been thinking that they're spending way too much time talking about the impeachment and very little time on anything else," he said. "It's *kabuki* theater at its finest!"

"Kabuki? Ha!" bellowed the General. "Carle that is a damn good assessment of what's going on."

"There is also a rumor floating that President Xi of China has been making some major changes within the People's Communist Party to maintain his seat at the table. His term will run through 2023, but the National People's Congress conveniently voted to end presidential term limits–virtually extending Xi's reign for life," the General said. "Carle, with the likelihood that Trump will be re-elected and the fact that he is making unilateral decisions on so many important constitutional issues, it seems that we may soon have three dictators ruling the world for the next four years at a minimum. Think about that!"

The General inched closer to Carle and talked softly,

"If that isn't enough to get you worried, don't you think this intrusion on our privacy and personal information through face recognition tracking is worrisome? We hear about how China uses it to blame and shame people for jaywalking or not paying their bills. And, we know that our government has been using the same technology for about a decade.

"You worried years ago during the Lakewood case about face recognition monitoring and controlling Black people. Don't you think that the more these companies learn about how to use face recognition technology for their benefit, the more they will try to use it? And, perhaps share it with the government? You guys were on to something back then, the thought of putting a value on a face was brilliant. It just took about two decades and the development of Facebook to monetize the concept!"

Carle sighed, reflecting on his time with Olivia and Nigel. He agreed with the General that they had been onto something in terms of the litigation to support the Lakewood High school district and parents, but they were completely naïve about where it would all eventually lead.

"That was Nigel's idea," Carle admitted. "He came up with it from his gap year in England looking at 17th and 18th century portraits."

"Well, I'll be damned," the General said.

Carle finished up his waffle and took a swig of coffee. Wiping his mouth with his napkin, he asked, "But, General, I'm still missing the piece of what I have to do with any of it?"

The General took a sip of his orange juice and asked, "Carle, what is the foundation of this great country?"

"That's easy. Democracy," Carle replied.

"Yes, but something else that is almost as equally important," the General said.

Carle reflected on his many college classes in business and said, "The economy?"

"Very good answer, but not quite," the General said. "The answer is capitalism."

"Ahh, yes. Good ole, Adam Smith," Carle agreed. "Let me see if I can remember his theory."

The General gave Carle some time to mull it over, wanting

Carle to make the connection about the problems that may unfold in the future.

"Okay," said Carle, "I think it relates to the value given in exchange for a service or a product. The agreed price must be determined by competition within a free market, not set by arbitrary or government direction."

"Yes, you are correct," the General said. "Capitalism has been the shining light for the success of the United States of America, even before the Revolutionary War. The resources of this country and how we turned those resources into valuable commodities has been one of the main reasons our economy and our unit of exchange, the dollar, sets the tone for global economic growth and weakness."

"Okay, I get that," said Carle.

"But," the General intervened, "what is the current thinking about capitalism today?"

Carle thought to himself, *there is a lot of shit going on in the world today.* "I'm drawing a blank here."

The General leaned towards Carle not wanting to disrupt the room again. He whispered,

"People are starting to think that capitalism is bad. They forget that capitalism is the driver for jobs, millions of jobs, in just the last five years. In fact, we have the lowest unemployment rate ever. But all you hear about is the inequality between the haves and have nots. Why? Well, because most Blacks and a large segment of the fly-over states have not participated in the 'Make America Great Again' stock rally. In fact, if you look at inflation-adjusted incomes and wealth, Black Americans are actually worse off than they were 20 years ago.

"Capitalism is just a tool that has been taken over by the

elites. Did you know the inequality of pay is at its most extreme level ever? The recent estimate for the CEO to employee salary ratio is 220 to 1. That's two hundred and twenty times the pay. It's crazy. No wonder we have poverty and crime in low income areas. All the money gets sucked away by the corporate big shots, who in turn slide some money under the table to the lobbyists, who then will hand that money over to some Senator or Congressman for special favors."

Carle could see that the General was getting worked up over this. However, he was still clueless as to why they were meeting.

"Yes, I've read all the articles and looked at the data," Carle said. "But, what does all this have to do with me?"

"Carle, it's not just a job these people deserve, its access to healthcare, daycare, food, and education," the General said. "The 99% will suffer and remain poor, and in the end we will all end up losing something. Do you know what that is?"

"No, sir. I don't," Carle said.

"Control," the General said. "Once they take all the money, then they can take control. With money comes power, and with power comes leverage. Leverage that can be wielded against us."

Carle stared at the General, thoughts whirling around in his head, "For what purpose?"

"To take our freedom," the General said. "Democracy and individual rights have formed the basis for freedom since the founding of our great Country. The freedom to choose, the freedom to love, the freedom to hate, the freedom to make ob-scene money, or the freedom to give it away. People governed by a democracy can choose their destiny. But that will all go away if we let them take it."

"We?" Carle said. "How do 'we' play into it?"

"Yes, Carle. You and I," the General said. "We need to provide the spark. We need to be the catalyst to make sure they fail."

"What catalyst?" Carle asked.

"Something big. I don't know what it is, but we probably need to make it soon. We will be the catalyst or die trying," the General said.

Carle was going along with the General until he said that 'die trying' part. He had already done his part trying to make a change and got almost four years in prison for it.

"General, I agree with a lot of what you are saying, but I'm not interested in anything that includes me dying," Carle said.

"Come on, Carle. You can't be afraid of dying for a cause," the General said. "Isn't that why you went into the legal profession? Isn't that why you spent three plus years in prison? To make a difference. To help your people?"

Carle was getting pissed now. He didn't like the tone of the General and the accusations about his beliefs. "Don't tell me what to think," Carle yelled. The few people in the dining section were taking notice and staring. Carle could feel their eyes looking at him. Judging him. Hating him. Condemning him.

"Carle, settle down," the General said. "What I'm saying is true, you do feel those things. And, now you have a chance to settle the score."

Carle looked at the General. "What do you mean settle the score?"

"And, by the way, dying was just an expression," the General said. "I don't plan on getting either one of us killed. But hear me out."

For the next hour Carle listened to the General outline his thinking about how they could settle the score. How they could get the American people, heck the world, to see that there had to be a change.

"Carle, it all has to do with what your friend Nigel came up with over two decades ago," the General said.

"And, what is that?" Carle said, a little agitated.

"The value of a person's face?" the General concluded.

CHAPTER 35

LAX Westin Hotel
Los Angeles, California
February 4, 2020

Clare sat back in the booth to get in position at the lobby restaurant. She had requested this booth, because she was pretty certain where the General was going to sit with Mr. Harper. But, to force the issue, she gave the hostess twenty bucks to sit them at a particular table.

She had learned that the General was flying out to meet with Mr. Harper from one of her sources. It had been divulged by accident, but Clare made it seem inconsequential, so as not to raise suspicion later. She hadn't heard from the General in almost a year and was wondering what he was up to. And, it had been an awfully long time since she dropped Mr. Harper off at the Westlake Hyatt.

Today she was dressed as a Hollywood celebrity. Big dark sunglasses, a floppy hat over her long red hair and a mishmash of clothing. And, to top it off, she had her mobile phone plastered to her ear, talking gibberish to no one in particular.

Right on cue she noticed the General come into the lobby. Looking as sharp and dignified as usual, he casually looked around taking an assessment of the crowd. Still the military bearing and awareness of surroundings permeated from his demeanor.

The General wandered over to the front desk, content with his surroundings. The clerk pointed towards the back to what she assumed was the restroom. No sooner had the General left then Carle arrived on the scene. Basically, going through the same process and maneuver, Mr. Harper stood off to the side in the main lobby area to wait. The General walked in from the back, and Clare could hear them speak. It appeared that Mr. Harper was not as elated to meet as much as the General. But, then again, Clare could understand given all the hardship and disappointment in his life.

As agreed, the hostess sat them at the table just down from where Clare was positioned. There was a clear line of sight with a couple of empty tables in between. Clare put down her phone so she could position her handbag on the table. The handbag was lying flat so that the opening was facing the General and Mr. Harper. Tucked snugly inside was a small high-definition camera trained directly at their table. The video feed from the camera coming to life on another mobile phone perched on her lap.

While she could make out some of their conversation, she would review the full content of the video later tonight to make sure that she did not miss anything. She wasn't quite sure what to expect from this meeting, but she needed some leverage against the General, and this was her only chance.

The hostess came over and asked if everything was okay. Clare nodded her head in agreement and slipped her another $20 for good measure. The hostess was cute and seemed a little more interested in Clare than just the money.

Clare reached out and lightly touched her hand. "Thank you." It didn't hurt to make friends in this town she thought. Clare picked up her phone for another phantom conversation. What nonsense would she talk about now?

Hello, is this Sister Mary Joseph?

This is Clare Marie; do you remember me?

Yes, that is correct, Clare Marie from Marseille.

I'm fine. It is so good to hear your voice. How long has it been?

Yes, good memory. It has been 30 years since I left St Clare's for university.

I thank you. I couldn't have gotten into the school without your help and encouragement.

I did very well, scoring high on my exams just like you said.

No, I did not go to medical school. I know, it was always a dream of mine, but when I took classes in biology, I realized that I did not have the passion for medicine.

Yes, I did ask a lot of questions about the body. You still remember after all these years!

In the end I got my baccalaureate in banking and finance. It was exciting to work for the Ministry of Finance for a couple of years, but I got bored and restless.

Yes, just like at St Clare. I could never sit still and was always getting into trouble.

No, I don't go to mass as much as I would like, but I am still devout although I express it in different ways now.

Sister Mary, do you remember when I asked you about whether God was a man or woman?

Yes, I remember you getting frustrated with me.

No, I didn't know that the Abbess knew about that.

But you know, that is why I am calling you.

No, not about the abbess, but about my question.

Whether God is man or woman...

I know the scriptures, and our faith must give us strength to believe that he is a man. But all my life I have wondered why we must believe in something that can't be proven.

God is not testing me, Sister Mary. God has enlightened me with knowledge and wisdom.

Sister Mary, I think I can prove what God looks like.

It is not the work of the Devil. It is driven by God's will. He wants me to show the world. To help Him gain their trust.

Don't get angry, Sister Mary. You must see that people don't believe in the Almighty. They question the Mystery, the Ascension...they question everything. They have come to question the holiness of the church. The sinners that have sprung from within have poisoned the believers. It is time that we show them that Jesus did exist and does exist within us, so we can believe in God.

How can we show that?

By giving him a real face, Sister Mary. Not a face from the scriptures, nor from the past, but a true face in keeping with the time. A face that has value for the very existence of our place on this planet and in this universe.

I am not speaking the Devil's word. I speak the truth, Sister Mary.

Clare looked around. The room came back into focus. She realized that her fantasized chat with Sister Mary had been a little too real. She had been in a trance, unaware what the General and Mr. Harper had been talking about.

Looking up, Clare noticed that the General and Mr. Harper had parted ways. The General headed out the hotel front door and Mr. Harper headed back towards the bathroom. Clare contemplated whether she should approach Mr. Harper when he returned. They might have more in common than they both realized.

The old two-story building stood near the intersection of the 101 and 110 Freeways in central Los Angeles. With its red brick tiles and off-white stucco, it looked unremarkable and unimportant in the City of Angels. Yet, it served an important mission in the *paschal mystery* of Christ.

For within this structure resided the obscure but influential Pious Disciples of the Divine Master. A group of devout sisters who lived a daily existence of contemplative living. They were a modern version of women of the gospel, who portrayed Mary in her mission of being mother and teacher of Jesus of Nazareth.

These sisters, wise in the ways of the church, were the keepers of the flame for Mary. To hold dear to the truth that Mary, a woman, had an important duty to bring the word of God to the twelve apostles who would spread the *paschal mystery* of Christ throughout the land.

Set back from the 101 Freeway, isolated from the filth and crime of Los Angeles, but not the constant drone of automobile traffic, these Pious Sisters went about their day celebrating their Eucharist life in a variety of ways. Some sisters maintained the garden which brought bountiful harvest for sustenance. Some sisters shared the spirit of God and His son through artistic endeavors. And, some spent time focused on matters of more importance–sisters like Clare Marie of Marseille.

Sister Constance entered the chapel from the back of the room. She headed up towards the front for her afternoon devotional. She could make out the dark red hair of her good friend, Sister Marie kneeling in prayer.

Sliding in next to Sister Marie, Constance Rivata kneeled to offer praise and prayer to the holy Father. "Amen," she said, sitting back onto the pew waiting for Sister Marie to finish.

"Welcome back, Sister," said Sister Constance. "It is good to see you back from your travels. Did you find the answer you were looking for?"

Clare crossed herself and sat back onto the pew, looking at Sister Constance with her side vision, she crossed her hands on her lap just as she was taught at the St Clare monastery many years ago.

"Hello, Sister Constance, thank you for your welcome," said Clare. "Yes, I did find answers to my question. Answers that I cannot believe and cannot wait to share with the world."

Sister Constance was Clare's closest friend at the 'Pious Centre,' as the sisters liked to joke about their humble quarters. A stark contrast from the massive mansion up the 101 freeway, known by most people, as the Church of Scientology Celebrity Centre. If only Tom Cruise had been a Catholic, they whispered.

Constance was only one of a few members of the servant disciples that knew about Clare and her calling—a calling that had been identified so long ago. It was a small circle, and one that has grown small over the years.

Sister Clare Marie was chosen by Canoness Lisieux of Perpignan, just after her 16th birthday, to unveil the *paschal mystery* of Jesus Christ to the world. It was her calling to learn the wisdom of those within and without the Church, to seek the knowledge of the physical and social sciences, to understand the finances that run church and state.

"Sister Clare Maire, you must bring Christ from the shadows for all to see. He can no longer be hidden from our eyes," Canoness Lisieux proclaimed. "The divine mystery of Christianity must be explained. Man and woman can now grasp the totality of his magnificence, his place in our world, as the son of God."

Clare kneeled before the Canoness within the small confines of the main chapel. The enormity of the words would not be understood until decades later. After her time at university, after the job in the Ministry, and even after the short spell in matrimony. For Clare new that her calling was ordained by God, just as her mother told her when she was abandoned at the monastery years ago.

"Rise, Clare Marie of Marseille, may the Lord our Savior guide you on your journey."

Canoness Lisieux leaned forward and gave Clare a kiss on each cheek, a gesture uncharacteristic of one of high standing. Whispering in Clare's ear, "Don't let us down, Clare Marie. Our survival depends on you. Do whatever it takes."

Surprised, Clare accepted the warm kiss with grace. She turned to share the joy with the small crowd in attendance. It was her time to shine under the gaze of Jesus Christ perched high atop the altar. Stepping towards the door, she turned one more time to look at his Face. Could it be that simple?

PART THIRTEEN

CHAPTER 36

Austin Hilton Hotel
March 13, 2021

I felt embarrassed crashing right into Olivia, but then again it had been rather good timing. It was going to be awkward anyway, so why not just get it out of the way. Walking away from the elevators, l scan the hotel lobby, looking for a familiar face. Unbeknownst to Clare, I have a shadow partner who tags along on these assignments. She is part of the clandestine branch out of the firm. This group is more concerned with real time command and control, and not so much the identification and documentation function of authenticators.

Faces and Aces–that is the name we use within the company for the two different teams. Looking around, l spy her. Tall, thin, long black hair. Always dressed in the latest trendy fashions.

Mae. A second generation Chinese American. Her grandparents had come to America with the first big migration after World War II. They settled in Chinatown in San Francisco, *straight off the boat* as her grandmother would say proudly. It didn't take them long to transition their skills as physicians in China into a network of medical clinics within the immigrant communities of the San Francisco Bay–a business that eventually was taken over by her parents.

With such a lineage for success, Mae had a high bar set for her at an early age. Educated at the best private schools in Pleasanton, California, and an undergrad at Stanford on a full academic scholarship, Mae had a charmed life, although it wasn't without hard work and drama.

She was encouraged to spend a year traveling around China to better understand her family legacy and learn how to do business in the China. She returned to the United States, not so enamored with the new China, despite the desires of her grandparents. The one thing she did learn on her year of travel was that the world was a lot different than what she had learned in school and watched on television. So, it was no surprise when she chose to pursue graduate work in International Policy at UC Berkeley.

The kid is a whiz-bang, and I couldn't believe my good fortune when Doc approached me about working with Mae on assignments. Mae is brilliant and quick of mind. She could get a high six-figure income on Wall Street or Sand Hill Road. Her academic accomplishments alone could open any door, but the connections of her family put her at another level altogether. To be working for me is a miracle or good fortune.

"Hi, Mae," l approach with a smile.

I tried early on to speak Cantonese, but Mae asked me to stop. She couldn't suffer through the butchering of the Chinese language.

"*Ni hao,*" Mae comments, looking at me over her face covering.

Oh, shit, I think. She is in one of those moods. "*Ni hao ma,*" l reply casually. "How are you doing, Mae?"

"I seek the truth. What have you seen today, face seeker?" Mae says looking at me with her big brown eyes. l stood there, stammering for something to say.

Suddenly, Mae burst out laughing. "Oh, man. I got you so bad, Nigel!" Mae shouts effusively. "I had you going that time. The look on your face. Classic."

"Yeah, classic alright," l comment. "Girl of Tiny Breasts."

"Zing, hitting under the belt already," Mae says, punching me in the shoulder.

It was a topic we discussed all the time. Mae so longed to have big boobs, so she could show off a little cleavage. But no, she has been stuck at 34A, ever since the 6th grade.

"Okay, okay. I'm sorry I went there too soon," l say. "But, I'm tired, and we've got things to do. Any news on the old guy from the airplane?" I ask.

"Yes, got the report this morning," Mae says. "Your spidey sense was correct. There is no record of this guy in our database."

"I knew it!" I say.

"What does HQ want us to do about it?" I ask.

Mae pulls her face covering down, reminding me how young my partner is for such a big task.

"They want me to tail him around the meeting and try to get him alone for a detain and obtain," she says.

"Oh, that's some pretty heavy shit," I say worriedly. "Are you ready for that?"

Mae looked around nervously, not wanting to reveal her fear and anxiety.

"I got this covered," she says turning and walking away. "Go see what Clare is up too."

Before I can ask what she means by that statement, she is gone. Her slim figure and slight stature blending in with the crowd. Wondering what in the hell she meant, I looked at my watch.

Crap. I was running late. I'll have to text Clare later.

CHAPTER 37

Olivia strides towards the speakers' room. Amazed that she didn't recognize Nigel, but then again, it had been a very long time. *How long?* she wonders. Let's see, they worked on the Lakewood case in about 1993, and she seemed to remember him hanging around a few years afterwards, so maybe 35 years.

"Hello, Ms. Vazquez!"

Startled out of her walk down memory lane, Oliva gasps. "What?"

"I'm sorry to have startled you," says a pleasant looking young man sporting an American flag face covering, wearing chinos, a plaid shirt, and a Patagonia puffer vest.

Oliva stops and takes a moment to collect herself. "No problem, I just ran into an old friend I haven't seen in decades," she says. "I was just daydreaming."

"That's okay. I understand completely. This conference is a great place to reconnect with friends and colleagues," says the young man. "In fact, I met my husband here three years ago."

"Umm. Well, good for you," responds Olivia.

"Well, you ready to review your presentation?" he says through the face covering.

"Yes, I would like that very much. My talk isn't for a couple of hours, but I want to make sure it is all set, and then run through the presentation one more time," Olivia comments, putting on her face cover.

"No problem, walk right over here to this computer station. I have it all booted up and ready to go," he says. "And, just to let you know I disinfected the keyboard and workspace from the prior user."

"Why, thank you. I appreciate a clean workspace. You are so professional," comments Olivia, "and I like your vest. Really cozy looking."

The young man beams with pride. "Thanks, my husband got it for me when he was up in Seattle last year. He's such a sweetheart."

"Sounds like a keeper to me," Olivia says.

"Oh, he is. And, in so many ways," he winks.

Olivia bows her head, trying to clear that vision from her mind. *Okay, focus on the presentation,* she thinks to herself. Olivia clicks on the folder tab and reads the list of files, looking for the SXSW2021 file.

One click and the PowerPoint pulled up. She had thought of using Prezi for something different, but she ran out of time. Nothing wrong with the gold standard of convention talks. Snooze.

Well, I will just have to spice this up with my wit and charm, Olivia chuckles inside, remembering the gazillion times when Alphonso informed her that juries did not like when defending counsel used humor or wit during a trial.

Alphonso was a good mentor, and she appreciated working with him and the firm for ten years. She had the good fortune to be on a great number of important civil liberty cases. But there comes a time when an attorney either stays *of counsel* or becomes *the counsel*.

And, for Olivia, she wanted to make a name for herself and her parents. They deserved that after everything they did to make her childhood safe and successful.

"Excuse me. Ms. Vasquez, right?" says a stern, older-looking woman wearing a black face mask and a pair of black gloves.

Olivia looks up. "Yes, I'm Olivia Vasquez."

"Hello. I'm Grace Epstein, the moderator for your panel discussion this afternoon," Stern Lady says.

Olivia politely stood up, refraining from the tendency to shake hands. "Hello. Nice to meet you."

"Yes. It is a great pleasure to meet you," Stern Lady says.

"You probably don't remember me, but I met you about 35 years ago. My uncle is Saul Rosenberg, and I would come to the office after school to help around the office. Mostly to get coffee and files, but I was able to sit in on discussions sometimes."

"Yes, I remember you. You were always so quick with a smile and a helping hand," Olivia replies.

Stern Lady smiles, "Why, thank you. I remember like it was yesterday when you pitched your summary statement for the Lakewood case. Inspiring."

"Well, gosh, thanks," sputters Olivia. "I haven't been flattered like that in a long time. But, go ahead, keep it up," she chuckles.

"Any time, girl. You deserve credit for warning about the civil liberty concerns about biometric recognition, long before it became a reality," Stern Lady says approvingly.

CHAPTER 38

Austin Hilton Hotel
March 13, 2021

The tricky part for Clare is going to be getting an automobile. Walking out through the main hotel entrance, Clare glances around hoping to find an easy target. Just as she is about to start walking towards downtown, a middle-aged man starts to climb into a black Chevy Malibu. Perfect. *Nothing like a standard corporate rental car to blend in*, Clare thought.

"Excuse me, sir," Clare says in her sultry French accent.

Looking down the street, she points and says, "I need ride to auto place."

Nothing wrong with using the French blonde routine to help move things along.

"Why, little lady, it would be my pleasure to help a damsel in distress," Middle-aged Guy grins strutting around to open the passenger car door.

"Merci, thank you." Clare replies.

"Sugar, you are going to make my day," Middle-aged Guy comments, closing the door.

Clare looks out the window as the car pulls away from the

hotel. She couldn't help but notice in the reflection from the window that the driver had his eyes more on her, than on the road.

Slowly, she turns to him, sliding her left arm along the seat and along his leg. "Why don't we make it a good day for us together," Clare whispers.

The car lurches to the left as Middle-aged Guy about jumps out of his seat.

"Be careful, baby. We don't want to die before we go to heaven," Clare coos.

"Yes, ma'am."

"There is a space," Clare says pointing up ahead and sliding her hand inside Middle-aged Guy's thigh.

"Just hold on, sugar. Don't get me too excited. I don't want to finish before we get started," he chuckles.

Middle-aged Guy pushes the speed up a little to change lanes. Turning the right blinker on, he looks for a driveway.

"Sugar, this doesn't look like an open space to me. It's an old car dealership."

"No problem, it looks good to me. We can go behind buildings," Clare breathes. "I am, how you say, excited."

Middle-aged Guy feels the heat and turns at the first driveway, heading back towards the old service entrance of the dealership.

"Park there," Clare points to an open area.

Middle-aged Guy sees what appears to be an old service bay. He navigates around some old boxes and a tool chest.

"Here we go, sugar. All nice and cozy, nobody can see us from the road," he snickers.

"Yes, very good idea," Clare says while pulling the Glock from her shoulder bag. "Now, get out."

"What the fuck?" Middle-aged Guy shouts, leaning towards Clare. "You bitch!"

Clare hits him on the forehead with the Glock handle.

"Christ! Why'd you do that?" he yells.

"Not nice to call me a bitch, asshole," Clare says. "You're lucky I don't shoot you in the nuts."

"Now, get the fuck out of the car, and put your hands on that wall, feet apart!" Clare yells.

Middle-aged Guy stumbles out of the car with his right hand covering the gash on his forehead. Blood streaming down his nose.

Clare got out on her side, keeping an eye on the asshole.

Middle-aged Guy is trembling, leaning on the wall with one hand, the other on his forehead.

"Don't kill me. I can give you money," he shouts, looking back towards Clare.

"I don't need your fucking money. I need to borrow your car for a few hours," Clare commands.

"Now, this is how it's going to go," she says in a low, calming voice. "I am going to take your car out for a few hours. You will not go to the police, or I will tell them that you drove me here and raped me."

"Okay, I won't. But what am I going to do?" Middle-aged Guy whimpers.

"That is your problem. I suggest you go find a Walgreens and get something for that gash. Then, hang around a Star-buck's for a couple of hours," Clare says. "I will park your car at the supermarket on Lamar Boulevard down the street later tonight. I will put the keys under the seat."

Middle-aged Guy stares back.

"Now, hand me your cell phone, so you don't do something

stupid."

He pauses, assessing his options.

Clare raises the Glock.

"Listen to me. Don't be stupid," she commands again. "I don't have time for this shit, so having you dead might be an easier solution."

Middle-aged Guy reaches into his coat pocket, throwing the phone at her. Wise to his plan, Clare steps aside and lets it sail across the service bay.

"You are losing points here, dipshit," Clare says, walking backwards to the phone, watching Middle-aged Guy.

Crunch! Clare's boot slams down on the phone, cracking the case and the screen.

"Now walk over to the back corner," Clare motions with the Glock.

Middle-aged Guy slowly moves to the back of the service bay. One hand up and one hand on his face.

How pathetic, Clare thinks. *Did he piss his pants?*

She slowly climbs into the car, the key still in the ignition. A quick start of the engine, one last threatening motion to the pathetic man, and she puts the car in reverse.

Having reversed and turned the car to the side. Clare looks at the guy who is now turned around staring at her. With the window down, Clare yells, "Next time, watch who you want to go to heaven with, asshole."

And, with that, she punches the gas and drives off. Now, time to pick up Carle and get to the hotel.

In a different part of Austin on the same day, the general wakes up at 5:00 AM.

Just like he did every morning for the past 40 years.

Standing over the toilet, he waits to pee. It seems like his kidneys are about the only things not working anymore.

"Fuck it," he shouts to nobody, stepping away from the toilet without much success.

A daily routine of 100 sit-ups, 50 push-ups, and 25 squat jumps keeps him lean and mean. Looking as fit as he did back at West Point. He crouches down onto the floor in his hotel room.

After he got out of West Point, he was stationed at Fort Bragg in North Carolina. His first commanding officer bestowed upon him the knowledge of the 100-50-25 program.

And, given that this Commanding Officer was the youngest officer to lead the Special Forces regiment with three bronze stars from Combat in Vietnam, the General, as an impressionable second lieutenant, soaked up as much from this true warrior as possible.

"93, 94, 95," the General counts his sit ups, hearing the familiar ping of a text message, "96, 97, 98, 99, 100."

The General leans over picking up the phone from the floor.

Another part of the warrior fitness routine is to keep the total time under 25 minutes. He takes a quick look at the screen to review the sender of the text. "Fuck that shit," he says throwing the phone to the side. Another one of the creditors trying to collect on his unpaid credit cards.

Ever since the death of Dorene and Margaret, he has spent a fortune for information about the World Trade Tower tragedy. After all these years, he still can't believe that the U.S. government knew about the terrorists and did nothing about it.

"1, 2, 3, 4," the pushups getting a little harder with advancing years. It seemed that his shoulders didn't quite like the punishment.

"22, 23, 24, 25," he stops and takes a quick rest, thinking about the day ahead, pushing on "26, 27, 28, 29…"

Another ring announces another text message.

"Jeezus Christ," he yells, breathing hard as he finishes the pushups "47, 48, 49, 50."

The General stands up, shaking his legs and arms. He raises his arms above his head stretching them way back, extending as far back as he can, breathing in and out, slowly.

With great reluctance he moves into position for the squat jumps. He squats down, pushing up forcefully with both legs. As he reaches peak height, he turns, landing in a crouching position, facing the opposite way. Again, he thrust himself up into the air to repeat the cycle again. "1" he counts, landing hard on his feet, crouching down.

Thinking of the time in the service of his country and the death of his wife and daughter always made him push harder during his morning exercise.

35 years. Twenty, of which, were a complete waste of time.

A series of chirps came from his phone. He takes a quick look.

The team is starting to come alive; he smiles.

"10, 11, 12, come on old man, you can do it," he yells to himself. "13, 14, 15, 16."

The phone buzzes, not a text message, but a real phone call.

"23, 24, 25," the General finishes, walking over to the phone.

Breathing heavy and hard, he answers, "MacCallum."

The General paces around the room, shaking his legs, breathing labored but controlled, listening to the voice on the other end of the phone.

"Affirmative," he responds, "Proceed with Operation Lightning Bolt."

CHAPTER 39

Austin Convention Center
March 13, 2021

L ate in the afternoon l rush out of the Lady Bird Johnson room hoping to get a good seat to watch Olivia's presentation. The session that just ended was about the use of the eigenface transformation for processing images within a face recognition software.

I remember the first time I heard the word, eigenface. It was my first day at the law firm back in 1993 and Olivia was reviewing our pending case on the Lakewood High School litigation. She mentioned the face recognition software being used by the Los Angeles Sheriff's Department, and I was hooked.

It was fuzzy to me then, and quite frankly it is still a bit fuzzy after Doc tried to explain it to me during my initial interview with him last month. However, the talk by Professor Jones out of the University of Texas mathematics department put it into better perspective: "The use of eigenface vectors is all about the storage size of an image and how that image can be standardized for comparison purposes within a data set."

Professor Jones started with a picture of an old cathode-ray tube television. Think of those old, gigantic televisions your grandparents had back in the day. They ran off raster scan display technology rather than vector display programming.

The difference is subtle but profound when thinking about storing an image on a tape drive or reproducing a television show. Basically, all images are stored as picture elements or pixels, depending upon the grey-scale light emitting through or reflected off the image.

Think of that old saying, 'white reflects sun rays and black absorbs them', which makes me wonder why my junior tackle football team had black helmets, black pants, and black jerseys. Not such a good idea in the California sunshine.

With a raster image, an electron beam will read from left to right, top to bottom, moving along a set line composed of dots that reflect whether the beam is on or off. The resulting image is a collection of X and Y coordinates that match up with the dots as either on or off. In practice, the electron beam is directed onto the monitor and follows the pattern as recorded from the original image resulting in a black and white television show or output on a data terminal.

Think of that computer monitor your parents purchased in the 1980s with the green text. The IBM 5151 was one of the most successful monitors of all time, although it had limited functionality compared to today's technology. With a resolution of 720 by 350, it pretty much allowed for simple text functions. Although in later years, graphic card adapters were developed for games like Pong.

The computer monitor systems were cumbersome and slow; they were held hostage by the storage capability of the screen image. The IBM 5151 and its 720 by 350 resolution would require 252,000 pixels. Today, for the streaming and gaming public, we have televisions with 4K technology, or 4096 x 2160-pixel resolution, requiring almost 9M pixels to be stored.

The limited storage function of the 1980's and 1990's meant that most monitors were of a single intensity with that eerie green glow. Now this was all fine and dandy for playing Pong or doing spreadsheet analysis, but the world was moving beyond standard photographic processes and into the digital world. And, to do that required a new type of thinking.

As Professor Jones outlined during his lecture:

"In 1988, Kirby and Sirovich showed how to transform all the pixels from an image and represent them as a two-dimensional graph utilizing principal component decomposition or the eigenface technique. This helped significantly reduce the number of data points required for storing images in digital format, when the cost for data storage was beyond most businesses and universities at the time.

"Later, following up on the work of Kirby and Sirovich, Turk and Pentland demonstrated how an unlikely variance component from the decomposition could be used for identifying images within a dataset. Moreover, the combined processing power of the eigenface technique could now be used for real time face recognition. An event that moved face recognition out of the academic laboratories and into the world of personal identification and revenue.

"Basically, instead of worrying about each individual pixel, the eigenface process uses linear algebra to determine the path or eigenvector...think geometry class...of the pixel image as it moves from lighter to darker shades within an image. The eigenvalue determines the magnitude of the transformation.

"To help make the data set manageable, the eigenface system

smooths the dataset by taking out the most common eigenvectors, leaving only those vectors that are unique to the image. So, instead of worrying about 1000's of vectors, we are left with an image that is composed of only 100 vectors."

Walking out of the Lady Bird Johnson conference room at the Austin Convention Center made me realize how forward-thinking and daunting the project being conducted by the Los Angeles Sheriff's Department had to be back in 1993.

The mathematics behind the eigenface functions were just being created, and both the storage and computer power of the day were extremely limited. I could understand the proprietary nature of the project, but I am still not quite certain how the Lakewood case became a national intelligence issue.

The settlement of the Lakewood case had come and gone so fast that we never had a chance to do any follow-up discussion as to the why. And, when Carle was terminated within a few months of the Lakewood settlement and then arrested a few years later for trying to share some of the information related to the case, it made the whole thing seem surreal.

Naturally, I occasionally think about the Lakewood case off and on. The abruptness of the settlement, the increasing use of face recognition in social media platforms for identifying people in photographs, and the use of face recognition for public shaming made it hard not to think about.

I bound down the escalator to the main floor of the convention center, noticeably excited to see Olivia. I bolt off the escalator and head straight to the Longhorn room down the next hallway. As I approach the room, I notice Olivia standing outside speaking to a woman wearing a black face mask.

"Well, that is crazy!" I hear Olivia say. "Why would anyone call in a bomb threat for my presentation?"

"I don't know," says the woman, "but they did specifically say the Longhorn ballroom."

With that news, I walk up to Olivia, "What's going on?"

Olivia jumps.

"Oops! Sorry, Olivia," I say. "I didn't mean to startle you!"

"It's okay, Nigel," Olivia comments. "I guess you haven't heard about the bomb threat. I'm a little jumpy."

I look at the woman. She seems familiar to me. "What's going on?" I ask.

The woman looks at Olivia. "It's okay, Grace."

"Well, about an hour ago, the convention center got a call regarding a bomb being placed in the Longhorn ballroom," Grace shares.

I look around, just now realizing the police officers with dogs heading into the Longhorn room.

"Wow, don't you think we should perhaps move outside?" I ask.

Both ladies look at me, agreeing as we turn and head towards the main lobby. Once outside, the woman pulls Olivia aside and whispers something in her ear.

"Okay, Grace. I'll see you later," Olivia says pulling Grace in close for a hug. Social distance be damned!

The woman turns and looks at me, "Nice seeing you again, Nigel," and walks away.

I stand there looking at Grace and Olivia. "She looks familiar to me, but I can't place her with that face mask," I say.

Olivia chuckles. "Yes, she is Saul Rosenberg's niece and sat in many of our meetings at CCR."

I stand there placing her covered face with my memory of her from CCR. "Oh, yeah. What is she doing here?"

"She is one of the organizers of my talk. I met her this morning," Olivia shares.

"Well, what a coincidence," I laugh, looking around. "I guess we might as well go get that drink now. Still interested?"

"You bet, and maybe more than one!" Olivia offers, "I'm pretty upset about this bomb threat. I don't get it, why my talk?"

"It is quite interesting," I say, "but I am getting a sense of *déjà vu* here!"

CHAPTER 40

Hyatt Place
Austin-Bergstrom International Airport
March 13, 2021

Clare pulls up to the entrance of Carle's hotel near the airport, hoping that he is ready to go, as they are running behind schedule. It is about a thirty-minute drive to downtown Austin and middle-aged guy wasted a lot of her time with his shenanigans.

Thankfully, Carle appears immediately through the hotel sliding doors and hops into the passenger front seat. "Hello, Chanel," Carle says, moving with purpose to gain control of the situation.

"Hello, Mr. Harper," Clare says softly in her French accent. "You don't wish to sit in back."

Carle gazes over at Clare. "No, I don't think we need to play the game of chauffeur anymore, do you?"

Clare looks at Carle assessing the situation.

"*Oui*, it is not needed. We are late for meeting," Clare responds, stepping on the gas. She casually observes Carle with her peripheral vision while looking in her rear-view mirror. He appears calm, but she senses some trepidation on his part.

Carle says off-handedly, "I can't determine whether you are friend or foe?"

"What means friend or foe?" Clare responds back.

"It means I don't know if I can trust you!" exclaims Carle.

Clare slowly turns her head towards Carle. "I take you to General. That is all," she says.

"I trust no one," Clare speaks, pushing on the gas. "Now, no more talk, we are late."

Olivia and I are standing in front of the Austin Convention Center on Trinity Street. People seemingly oblivious to the bomb threat 500 feet away.

"It still seems very curious that your talk would elicit a bomb threat," I say.

"I agree," Olivia says nodding in agreement. "It was just going to be a generic overview of privacy laws and personal identification. I can't think of anything in the program description that would incite someone that much."

"Are they going to reschedule your talk?" I ask.

"They don't know, it all depends on what they find with their search of the room and review of any tangible evidence from around town," Olivia comments.

Looking around the area for any clues, I shake my head. "I don't get it. There doesn't appear to be anything out of the ordinary here," motioning around. "You don't see police barricades with protesters waving signs and banners about privacy rights."

I look up and spy the JW Marriott across the street looming above us. "Well, not much we can do about it now. Let's go over to the Marriott and catch a late lunch," l ask.

"Might as well," Olivia responds.

Walking along East Second Street, Olivia and I get caught up on our past lives.

"You mean after leaving the firm you lost interest in the legal profession?" Olivia exclaims.

"Yes, it was exhilarating to work on the Lakewood case with you, but I eventually realized I didn't like the nuances of interpreting the law."

"It can be a bit challenging and frustrating," Olivia shares. "I must say there have been many times when I question whether what I was doing actually benefited people or hurt them."

"What you have done after Lakewood is phenomenal," I tell Olivia. "Your writings regarding the basis of personal rights on all matters related to self, and in particular health, helped lay the framework for the Health Insurance Portability and Accountability Act of 1996."

Olivia smiles. "Yes, I am quite proud of that piece of legislation. It really helped shed light on the dangers related to personal health information floating around on the world wide web, as we called it back in the day," she chuckles. "I am most appreciative of the work of Professor Susan Barnes out of Rochester Institute of Technology."

"Yes, I remember seeing her name in several of your papers I read flying over from San Diego," I comment. "Little did we know that our work on the Lakewood case was an early peek into the future of privacy and government intrusion."

"And, don't forget corporate snooping," Olivia says.

"Yes, it's hard to determine which is the lesser of two evils," I confide.

Walking with Olivia to the Marriott I remember a conversation that I had with Carle just before he got out of Lompoc.

"You are not going to believe the book that I tracked down on the Internet," Carle said.

"What?" I asked, watching his excitement.

"A book that was published in 1986 and talked about the information society. It's called, *The Control Revolution*," Carle said. "It outlines the many advances in manufacturing and transportation during the Industrial Revolution between 1850 and 1914; it contrasts them with the advances we are experiencing today with improved microprocessors and telecommunications."

"Really? That sounds like quite the book," I commented.

"No, man I'm telling you straight up," Carle said. "What this guy wrote in 1986 is happening now. Big Brother has arrived, and it has a new name—the Internet," he said. "It's not what George Orwell envisioned, but pretty darned close. Instead of the government watching and taking control, it's companies tracking every click of our mouse and then selling the aggregate click data to the highest bidder."

Holding the door open so Olivia could enter the Marriott, Carle's statement years ago made me realize how prescient his statement was, but now we call it *Social Media*!

Clare pulls into the car entrance on East Third Avenue of the JW Marriott.

"We park with valet, then meet the General," she turns looking at Carle.

"Whatever you say, Chanel," Carle responds.

Putting the car in park, she steps out of the car, handing the car key to the attendant. "Take good care of car, it is friends," Clare requests.

"Yes, ma'am," the young attendant says, taking a nice long look at the blonde. Clare smiles watching the young man checking her out.

"Wait, Mr. Harper," she yells scooting around the car towards the revolving door. Carle waits patiently inside. Clare steps through the revolving door reaching into her bag.

Pulling out her mobile phone, she checks for messages. "General say we go down one floor. Then we look for fitness center."

Carle looks around for anything suspicious. Nothing seems out of the ordinary. There are no federal agents waiting for him this time. Carle motions to Clare to follow him down the hallway towards the escalator, just as Nigel and Olivia enter the hotel across the lobby.

PART FOURTEEN

CHAPTER 41

JW Marriott Hotel
Austin, Texas
March 13, 2021

"**E**xcuse me." I lean over the table and tell Olivia. "I need to go to the bathroom."

"Okay, I'll just check to see if they have resolved the problem for my talk." She replies.

I look around the bar for anything that indicates where the restrooms are located.

"Can I help you, sir?" says the server, wearing a black smock dress and a very fashionable face covering. I look at her. I must be getting older because this gal looks way too young to work in a bar.

"Umm, yes. Where are your restrooms?" I ask.

Her dark brown eyes look at me over her face covering. "Straight ahead by that sign that says 'restroom."

"Oops. Must be the eyes." I reply.

"No problem. Happens all the time." She comments, letting me off the hook. "We often make observational errors in unfamiliar places."

I am struck by the significance of her comment. Her statement forms the most basic tenet of face recognition pattern strategies.

It is easy to find a target face in a database containing a verified image of the face. With enough computing power and time, eventually the math behind the program can provide a list of images that match the target.

But it is difficult to match an unknown face in a database containing 100 million facial images pulled from cameras around the world. Kind of like the card game where the magician asks you to pick out a card, look at the card, and then slip it back into the 52-card deck. The magician shuffles the cards, waves her hands around the deck, and then slowly spreads the cards out on top of the counter. What you are not noticing is that she is looking for the card that she marked in a deck of cards that she has memorized.

The success of the trick would be less than exciting if you were to pull out a card from her deck and place it into a card deck of your choosing. In this case, she would know that there is a card but not the pool of cards from which it was taken. In probabilistic terms this is referred to as the Hidden Markov Model defined as:

> "When a state or condition is unknown, we can make inference of said state through the probability of the observable state or conditions."

Basically, take the show *Let's Make a Deal*, the contestant can see three doors, but they don't know what is behind those doors. They only know that Monty told them that behind one of them was this fabulous travel package to Hawaii. The contestant knows the observable state or outcome—Hawaii, but they don't know which door leads to the prize. They must guess with a one in three chance of success.

The problem facing law enforcement is being able to correctly identify criminal suspects from an observed face in the crowd by matching it with an image that could be behind an infinite number of doors.

Even the most advanced face recognition systems have challenges, often with error rates far beyond acceptability for legal action. Now, given social distancing and face covering requirements related to the COVID-19 virus, law enforcement is finding it even more difficult to find an image. Even when the door is known. This is where the value of a super-recognizer like me comes into play.

"Nigel, did you go to the bathroom yet!" Olivia queries, snapping me out of my trance.

"Umm, no. I was just thinking about something the server said about error rates and unfamiliar places," I offer. "It reminded me of when Carle and I had our photographs scanned and matched in the Los Angeles Sheriff's department."

"Well, hurry up," Olivia says, "so we can reminisce together."

Carle and Clare glide along the hallway of the JW Marriott. "Why did the General move the meeting to the hotel?" Carle says as they approach the escalator going down towards the fitness center.

"You need to ask General," Clare says, "My job is to bring you here."

Carle lets Clare go first down the escalator and looks around to make sure they are not being followed. They step off the escalator and see that there appears to be a lot more going on than just the fitness center. The lobby is full of people. Carle looks at the crowd and wonders what the hell is going on.

"What is NRA?" asks Clare looking at a big banner hanging down from the ceiling of the lobby.

"National Rifle Association," says Carle, thinking that the General has something else planned than a meeting.

Together they walk through the crowd heading towards the fitness center. As they approach, the General steps out from the shadows. As usual, he is dressed in a bespoke business suit with a dark red and blue tie over a white shirt, looking squared away and ready for battle, just like he did when in the U.S. Army.

"Carle, good to see you," the General says extending his arm for a handshake," and, Chanel, good to see you as well."

"What in the hell is going on here?" Carle waves his arms around pointing to the crowd.

The General blows out a big laugh. "You don't appreciate my sense of humor?" he bellows.

l might be good with face recognition, but I was never one for directions. Evidently, I missed the restroom within the bar and found myself out in the hotel lobby. Those damn plexiglass panels.

Walking further down the hallway, I stumble upon a bank of restrooms for hotel guests. Luckily, there isn't a line because

I glance at the poster near the entrance, "Only four guests at a time. Thank you for understanding." That would be a real bummer if you really had to take a piss.

Inside I could tell that the bathroom had recently gone through a renovation to meet Federal guidelines. No more urinals, just individual stalls. I mean really, like guys are high fiving each other as they stand taking a whiz.

As I step back out into the hallway, l look around to get my bearings. I spot a guy that looks like Carle walking towards the escalator. Surprised that Carle might be here, l head towards the escalator to get a closer look. Still not sure whether it is Carle or not, l find myself in a dilemma. *Should I follow and make sure or go back and check in with Olivia?* The thought of Carle being here at the hotel gets the best of me—I had to know for sure.

Olivia looks down at the text from the conference coordinator apologizing for the cancellation and to let her know that they were not going to reschedule. No sense hanging around here. She had papers to grade for her legal ethics class at Pepperdine. She sends Nigel a quick text apologizing for her departure and the invitation to get together in the future. As she steps out onto Brazos Street to walk back to her hotel, she does not hear the ping of Nigel's text,

```
Sorry, but I think Carle is in the hotel and
in trouble. Wait for me!
```

CHAPTER 42

JW Marriott Hotel
Austin, Texas
March 13, 2021

I finish the text to Olivia and step onto the escalator heading down. I am fairly sure that it is Carle. And, it appears that he is in trouble. There's something about the way he is looking around. I need to find out what's going on.

Stepping off the escalator, I can't make sense of it. The lobby is full of people milling around. Spread around the room are vendor tables, and on one side, people are looking at tactical gear, hats, gloves, and uniforms. On the other side, I see something a little more troubling.

Weapons, all kinds of weapons: handguns, rifles, knives, and ammunition. Laid out before me is a flea market for not only law enforcement but those who take serious consideration of the Second Amendment: the right of the people to keep and bear arms.

I am trying to get a bearing on which direction Carle would have gone. Luckily, I don't have to look too far because I can see Carle up ahead talking with some old guy. And, now as I walk towards them, the old guy seems remarkably familiar. *Big ears, fit and trim, wide eyes with brown shades, short, military cut hair.*

I can't believe it when it dawns on me that he is the old guy from the airport. This just doesn't make any sense. Looking at him I still don't get a feeling that any of his biometrics fit within our database. I wonder what the heck is going on here.

Approaching slowly and from behind a group of NRA people, I try to listen in to what Carle is saying.

Carle looks at the General and says, "What's up with the NRA convention?"

"Don't you get it?" The General replies.

"Not really," Carle says. "I don't see what the NRA has to do with our plan,"

"They are just one of the many mouthpieces that are used to spin the story, don't you see?" The General says.

"The elitist sons of bitches have been fooling us about everything—the Middle East, sham oil embargoes, racial injustice, and the stock market. Now with the coronavirus pandemic they've been able to take what they have sought for so long—our freedom. Basically, house arrest for the country, heck, the world for that matter.

"My wife and daughter died because of them. Your people have suffered for 400 years because of them, and now the middle-class has been pretty much eliminated because of them. Now is the time to wake up the world to their corruption and dishonesty. And, you Carle are a big part of that 'wake up' call."

Carle looks over to Chanel wondering if she understands what is going on.

"What better place to announce that the U.S. government has been lying about the JFK assassination, the Oklahoma City bombing, the World Trade Tower terrorist attack, the wars in Iraq and Afghanistan, and this COVID pandemic," the General says, "than right here in front of these law abiding citizens who hold our constitutional rights near and dear to their hearts. The right to bear arms and protect our personal rights and privileges! Our freedom!"

"I'm sorry, General, but I'm still missing the big picture here. How does it fit with our discussions about the Presidential election and Russian meddling? Isn't that why you had me come here?"

"There needs to be a catalyst, Carle," the General says, "to get all Americans to rise up and take back our government."

Carle understood the catalyst part. He and the General have talked about this ever since he got out of Lompoc and in earnest over the past two months.

"I thought we were going to show how the Russians were helping the President divide the country even further apart, so he could get elected again?" Carle asks.

"It's still the plan, Carle," the General replies. "However, there has been a little change in who delivers the message."

"What do you mean 'who delivers the message'?" says Carle.

"General, we need to move," Chanel chimes in.

They look around and see a group of people walking towards them, oblivious to the heated conversation in front of them.

"Okay, let's move into the fitness center," the General says, "and I will tell you."

Standing off to the side, I get a good look at Carle and the old guy, but now I notice a blonde woman that appears to be with them. I can't hear anything they are saying, but my super-reg sensor is pinging that something isn't quite right.

I move up with the crowd and watch them head into the fitness center. I'm about to step out from the crowd when I see the blonde look back towards the lobby. The blonde wig and make-up provide some camouflage, but my amygdala kicks into gear to provide context.

I can't believe my eyes, but it's Clare! What in the hell is she doing here? I definitely need to find out what the fuck is going on now. I slowly approach the fitness center and quietly slip through the door.

Carle and the old guy are in the center of the room, and they are standing near the fitness equipment. Off to one side is a small area with wall mirrors and mats presumably for stretching and yoga, where I presume Clare to be.

"General, what's this about delivering the message?" Carle asks again.

Before stepping much further I hear, "Mr. Grant, welcome to the party!"

I step away from the door and look around. This old guy and Carle are in close quarters near the weight machines. I can't see Clare, but I do notice that the old guy has a gun pointing at Carle.

"Carle, what's going on here?" I ask stepping towards them being mindful that Clare is hiding.

"Well, I was just about to review that with Carle here," the old guy says.

"Nigel, be careful. The General is crazy," Carle says. "He was responsible for the Lakewood case being classified as top secret."

"I'm not crazy," says the General, "and yeah, truth be told, I was the one who convinced the Attorney General to classify the Lakewood case under the government secrets act."

"It was you?" I question.

"It was part of my job," he says, "but let me tell you a little about what I have planned for the two of you."

I step forward towards the General, thinking I could distract him so that Carle could karate chop his arm or something. Perhaps not realistic, but it seems to work in the movies.

"Nigel baby, don't do anything stupid," Clare says stepping from out of view.

Carle and I both look at Clare, perplexed. I'm wondering what in the hell is she doing here, and in those clothes. Carle, on the other hand, can't believe what he just heard.

"You know her?" Carle and I say at the same time.

"Jinx," the General says. We all look at the him.

"Hey, you said the same thing," he laughs. "Amazing you never figured out you were being played."

I place my hand on the treadmill to steady myself. I never had the chance to eat and the coffee is wearing off. Clare is positioned off to my right across from Carle and the General. It becomes evident that she is aligned somehow with the old guy. But I'm not quite sure why.

"How are we being played?" I say.

"Thought you'd never ask," the General says. "Without boring you on the details, I really thought this project was in the shit can until Chanel mentioned that you, Nigel, were working at Face Value."

Chanel, I think. How in the hell is Clare mixed up with this guy?

"It was like divine intervention. The heavens whispering in my ears that I now had the means from which to make a statement," the General says, "a statement choreographed by Carle and delivered by you!"

"Excuse me. I don't know what you're talking about," I reply. "And, how does Face Value fit into this mess?"

"Nigel, from what I can tell, you are a standup guy," the General says, "but you have been pretty naïve thinking that what you and Face Value are doing is legit."

Oh, oh, my head is spinning again. I don't know if I can take any more surprises. "What do you mean?"

"Did Doc ever tell you where he went for graduate school?" he says.

"Umm, not that I recall," I reply. "Why does it matter?"

"The University of Illinois," the General says, "one of the leading computer science and artificial learning centers."

Carle takes a step towards the old guy. "Carle, don't even think about it," Clare says raising her gun.

"Yeah, Carle," the General says. "You might find this of interest,

"Doc Gallegos was part of the research team that developed a program for analyzing air bubble formation within liquids, particularly oil, for the petroleum industry. Evidently, during the manufacturing process and transport through pipes, there is a problem with air bubble formation. This bubble formation leads to inefficiency of flow along with an increase in pressure within the system. The University of Illinois group was able to develop a real-time system for analyzing bubble formation to determine when there might be an emergent event. They were eventually able to achieve almost 95% prediction which significantly improved efficiency and reduced downtime due to maintenance and safety issues.

"Eventually, the University of Illinois reached out to other organizations for funding and came across a request for proposal from the DEA regarding pixel tracking within digital photography. They felt the pattern of air bubble formation within the cross-section of a pipe was like the change in pixilation color observed with digital photography. The field of biometrics and face recognition was still in its infancy, but the U of Illinois technology looked promising.

"Doc Gallegos took over the project and slowly changed the focus from real-time target acquisition towards more of a predictive tool. This was in 1998, and the DEA was being overwhelmed with the flow of drugs coming up from South America through Florida. Doc Gallegos proposed the idea to use their early systems at the Miami airport. The main goal was to try and identify known cartel members who were traveling on forged passports. Once an individual was identified, a secondary goal was to try determining intent, which Doc Gallegos labeled as behavior, with the individuals tracked throughout their time within the airport. For this goal, they looked at the target images compared against random images within the field of vision. The system was tested in the late 1990's at the Miami International Airport with great success."

"Yeah, I know that story," Carle yells. "So, what does that have to do with me and Nigel?"

"Don't be so impatient, Carle," the General says. "I'm pretty certain Nigel has never heard that story before!"

We were all getting a little antsy standing around in the fitness center. I looked over at Clare, still wondering how she fit into all of this. "Clare, what the hell is going on?" I ask.

"Sweetie, just listen to the General," Clare says. "It is for your own good."

I look at her, confused by her answer.

"Nigel, let me continue. We need to wrap this up, but I want you to understand the significance of what your work at Face Value means for personal privacy and surveillance detection."

The General continues,

"The face recognition system utilized in Miami was extremely successful and identified almost 94% of the cartel members trying to sneak into this country. The information of most interest ended up being the secondary outcome, which was intent. Just by tracking the target image of a cartel member over time, the University of Illinois system was able to demonstrate a high confidence that the target image exhibited different behavior than a random image.

"The DEA and the University of Illinois suggested that their system should be implemented throughout the country at all major ports of entry in the United States. However, due to a political divide between the DEA and the Department of Justice, the proposal was shelved as a matter of government secrecy. The DOJ was uncomfortable with anything related to face recognition and civil liberties at the time.

"Doc Gallegos felt that they could go further and identify people that had criminal tendencies. He eventually left the university and with funding from the DEA and DARPA set up Face Value with the goal to further refine the predictive qualities of the technology."

"I still don't get it," I look at Carle, "how does the World Trade Tower tragedy relate to any of this?"

"The system that was being tested at the Los Angeles Sheriff's

Department was a similar system to the one being tested in Miami," Carle says.

"So, what?" I say.

The General chimes in,

"So what? Don't you get it? If Carle had been successful in getting the face recognition software released for use in the Rodney King criminal trial, the police officers would have been convicted, and he more than likely wouldn't have gone to prison.

"And, if the DEA software had been implemented, the terrorists of the World Trade Tower bombing would have been identified upon entry to the country. And, my wife and daughter would still be alive!"

The General is distracted for a moment by a noise coming from the NRA convention lobby. Seeing an opening Carle lunges at him. But before he can make contact, Clare shoots him.

I stare at her and then at Carle who is lying on the ground. I can't believe what's happening, but I rush towards the General outraged. He gracefully side-steps my charge and punches me in the stomach. I bend over in pain with air escaping from my mouth…*ooofff*. Then he tags me on my chin and the lights go out.

CHAPTER 43

JW Marriott Hotel
Austin, Texas
March 13, 2021

Mae glides down the escalator to the lower level mezzanine. She has been following the old guy ever since headquarters confirmed that he wasn't in the database. Stepping off the escalator, she is struck by the number of people milling around. A good number are in Army fatigues from top to bottom, but the majority are wearing the casual look of someone who shops at Cabela's.

Mae has been given the green light to detain and obtain the old fart but hadn't planned on having a large audience. "Detain & Obtain" is the highest level of authentication in their system, and quite frankly, Mae has never actually done a D & O before. She is a little nervous but was assured by her senior manager that support is on its way. All she has to do is keep the old guy contained, so that he can't escape.

Mae peers around the pillar trying to figure out where they have gone. She has been watching the old guy talking with some Black dude and a stylish looking blonde. She is about to move closer when Nigel comes into view. *What in the hell is he doing here?*

He must have been hidden in the crowd because she hadn't seen him. This has gotten incrementally harder with the addition of Nigel. One thing that she has been taught at Face Value is to never allow harm to come to an authenticator.

Mae moves along the wall opposite of Nigel, keeping an eye on him and looking to see where the old guy has gone. However, it appears that Nigel is heading towards the fitness center, so Mae adjusts her trajectory to fall in close behind.

Mae watches as Nigel cautiously slips into the fitness center. *Where in the hell is the support team?* Mae looks down to see that she has zero bars on her mobile phone and decides to try the hotel Wi-Fi system.

Nigel has been in there for about 10 minutes, and Mae is getting worried. As she waits for the hotel Wi-Fi link to show up on her phone, Mae hears a gunshot. The loud noise carries throughout the small mezzanine room causing pandemonium. Hotel guests and NRA members alike are thrown into chaos, some running for cover and others pulling out their own weapons.

Mae is frozen as to what to do when the door of the fitness center bursts open. Out runs the old guy. Without thinking, Mae steps out and yells, "Freeze!" raising her Taser.

The old guy looks surprised to see her, raising his gun to fire. The part that Mae would never know is who shot that fatal bullet. The old guy did raise his gun, but he did not fire. That misfortune belonged to an off-duty police officer from Lubbock, Texas, in town to attend the NRA meeting.

The General lowers his gun, shocked by the scene that has unfolded before him. He looks at the young Asian girl splayed out on the floor. Like Margaret, too young to die.

I struggle to regain consciousness. The proverbial light at the end of the tunnel is true. I can see it down the way, although it kind of reminds me of something I once saw in the Sistine Chapel. Sunlight poking through a blue sky of wispy clouds all framed by a gilded doorframe.

"Nigel, wake up," I hear. Opening my eyes, I see Clare kneeling over me. My eyes slowly focus. Then I realize she's placing my hand around something.

"What are you doing?" I shout, trying to make sense of it all.

"Making sure your fingerprints are on the gun," she says.

"What gun?" I say.

"The one that shot Carle," she sighs.

"Clare, No," I shout. "Why Carle?"

"I know it's disappointing to you," Clare says kissing me on my cheek. "But you need to be strong for me. Okay!"

I'm getting angry now. Not liking where this is headed. "What the fuck, Clare?" I yell. "Who are you?"

"Don't worry about me, Nigel," she says. "Worry about Doc and what Face Value is doing with all the information you and all the other *super-regs* have been providing to his face recognition system."

Again, my head begins to spin. "I don't understand?" I say.

"You will," she says. "in time!"

I look at Clare. Wondering who this person is. Crying out in pain and despair.

"Ah, baby. Don't cry," she says. "Context, that's what it's all about."

"What about context?" I ask, thinking of her betrayal.

"You've helped Doc figure out how to incorporate 'context' into the face recognition system." She says.

"So what?" I say.

"Because they want to do more than just identify people, Nigel," Clare says standing up and looking down at me. "They want to utilize face images collected from around the world to build a database system that can learn whether a person will be good or bad. Passive or aggressive," she says pulling off the blonde wig and slipping on a long raincoat. "Then they will start eliminating them—one by one."

"That's crazy," I say.

"No, it's not," Clare says. "When you want total control of the world, it makes perfect sense. You need to get rid of those who will not be controlled."

"Clare, don't do this," I plead. "Stay here and help me."

I try to stand. It is difficult to breathe, and blood is running down my face. I'm a bit dizzy, but I need to face her. To show her that I am strong.

"It's been fun, sweetie," she says. "But I've got a plane to catch, and you won't be coming along."

With that she pulls a gun out of her coat pocket and shoots me in the shoulder. I fall back to the ground, pain shooting through my body like electricity.

"But, why" l yell as she heads out the door, "are YOU doing this?

Clare turns back to look at me one more time and whispers under her breath, *"Sui praesentia mea ut reveletur."*

His presence will soon be revealed!

ABOUT THE AUTHOR

Robert Hesslink is an independent financial advisor and adjunct professor living in Portland, Oregon with his family.

Intrigued by the survivalist movement out of Southern Oregon, Robert wrote his first non-fiction book entitled *Survival Fitness* in 1982, while working on his master's degree at Portland State University. It was written for individuals looking to survive from an attack by the Soviet Union--an attack that never came and a book that, sadly, never got published.

An interest in writing soon returned after Robert moved back to Portland in 2014. Noticing that many of his investment clients suffered from preventable chronic diseases, Robert decided to apply his experience in life science research to write a book about the value of three simple health behaviors. His book, *Eat Less, Sleep More, and Slow Down*, has been well received with Robert appearing on KGW Channel 8 and a write-up in the *Lake Oswego Review*.

Robert's venture in fiction storytelling, *At Face Value*, began in the summer of 2019 while traveling in Japan. The presence of smart phones in daily life and the intrusion of facial recognition from private and public industry sparked an idea: an idea about the dangers of facial recognition and the loss of personal privacy and freedom.